XOXO

XOXO

SWEET AND
SEXY ROMANCE

EDITED BY
KRISTINA WRIGHT

CLEiS
PRESS

Published in the United States by Cleis Press, Inc., 2246 Sixth Street, Berkeley, California 94710.

Printed in the United States.
Cover design: Scott Idleman/Blink
Cover photograph: © Ocean/Corbis
Text design: Frank Wiedemann

First Edition.
10 9 8 7 6 5 4 3 2 1

Trade paper ISBN: 978-1-62778-006-3
E-book ISBN: 978-1-62778-019-3

Contents

vii   *Introduction: Love Bites*

1   *Midnight* • EMERALD
6   *Soldier Boy* • SOMMER MARSDEN
11   *Anniversary Wrappings* • KATHLEEN TUDOR
16   *Because He Knows Her So Well* • SASKIA WALKER
22   *Control* • A. J. LYLE
28   *Unsnubbed* • JEREMY EDWARDS
34   *Designated Driver* • HEIDI CHAMPA
39   *Friend of the Court* • KELLY RAND
45   *Ouch!* • LILY K. CHO
51   *Steam* • MARIPOSA CRUZ
57   *The War at Home* • GISELLE RENARDE
63   *By the Sea* • ANGELA R. SARGENTI
68   *Gargoyle Lovers* • SACCHI GREEN
73   *Best Friends* • CATHERINE PAULSSEN
79   *Dirty Laundry* • MARTHA DAVIS
84   *Night Moves* • CHRISTINE D'ABO
89   *Miss Organized* • ELIZABETH COLDWELL
94   *When the Vacation Is Over* • ANNABETH LEONG
100   *The "Tilly" Crown Affair* • MICHAEL M. JONES
106   *Gentle Teasing* • RAELYNN MACDONALD
111   *Eighty Cupcakes* • NEVE BLACK
117   *Company Picnic* • ANYA M. WASSENBERG
122   *Imagination at Play* • BRIGHTON WALSH
127   *Heighten the Senses* • HEIDI CHAMPA
132   *Bathroom Play* • CATHERINE PAULSSEN
137   *Homecoming* • JENNA BRIGHT

142 *Simmering Down* • KATHLEEN TUDOR
147 *Nailed* • GISELLE RENARDE
153 *Perk of the Job* • CHEYENNE BLUE
159 *A.M. Wood* • ROSALÍA ZIZZO
164 *Steal the Key* • AMY GLANCES
170 *One Hot Wet Night* • VERONICA WILDE
176 *The Distraction* • LOUISE HOOKER
182 *Connecting Flight* • SALOME WILDE
188 *Wild Naked Bandits Flee the Square Conspiracy*
     • NIKKI MAGENNIS
195 *Faded Goods* • VIDA BAILEY
202 *Puzzle Pieces* • RACHEL KRAMER BUSSEL
207 *Very, Very Well* • KRISTINA WRIGHT

215 *About the Authors*
221 *About the Editor*

INTRODUCTION: LOVE BITES

I love a good love story, especially when it's one wrapped up in a sexy red bow. Erotic love, the kind that makes your heart beat faster and does exciting things a bit farther south, is what *xoxo* is all about. Like the candy hearts that are so ubiquitous around Valentine's Day, these sweet little sensual snippets are meant to tease you—and please you. In fact, it was the candy that inspired the idea for this collection. I wondered, as writers often do, why those popular little hearts are only available for such a brief time each year. Everyone loves them, so why can't we get them all year long?

And so, an idea was born. I can't give you the sugary sweetness of a BE MINE or TRU LUV candy heart, but I can present you with nearly forty stories that serve a similar delicious purpose—to remind you of the sweetness of love, the sharp bite of passion, the delight of discovering a favorite treat anew. *xoxo* is about old lovers and new lovers, lovers exploring each other in new ways and in ways that are tried and true. The stories each have their own kind of sweetness—and Emerald's well-timed

"Midnight" opens the collection with a romantic tradition that will inspire an *ooh!* as well as an *aw!*—but none of them are cloying. In fact, some of them have more than a little spice, such as Elizabeth Coldwell's stinging example, "Miss Organized."

These are stories of fantasy and desire—lovers capturing a single moment in time, much like you might capture a sweet candy on your tongue, savoring the taste of desire for as long as it lasts. It's not all about the sex (oh, but the sex is quite delicious!); there is love here, too. Love that overcomes long separations, such as the one in Sommer Marsden's summer delight, "Soldier Boy," and love that conquers physical limitations, as in Heidi Champa's poignantly kinky "Heighten the Senses." It's love that gets—and keeps—these couples together, and sometimes it's great sex that is the key to overcoming obstacles.

Every February, I find myself sifting through a box of multi-hued candy hearts, selecting the ones I like best before popping them in my mouth. I invite you to explore *xoxo* in the same fashion—shuffle through these sweet stories and discover the ones that you like best. And, as with those sweet Valentine indulgences, I hope you will be inspired to share your favorites with a lover. Or give him or her a box—I mean a book!—of their very own.

I'm thrilled to share my candy-inspired collection of sexy confections with you, dear reader. Sweet and sexy reading!

In love in Virginia,
Kristina Wright

MIDNIGHT

Emerald

S ometimes he's inside me. Sometimes my mouth is on his cock. Sometimes his tongue is against my clit or my nipple or whatever square inch of skin he's found that lights up that fire that's somehow inside me and outside me and everywhere else all at once.

It's different each time. But whatever form it's taking, sex is what we're doing. The timing is the important thing.

The waitstaff at the fondue restaurant converges on our table, singing "Happy Birthday" in charming unison as the single candle in one of the bite-sized pieces of pound cake in front of me is lit. I smile and thank them before blowing it out, earning a smattering of applause before the staff disperses amidst a chorus of well-wishes.

Matthew smiles at me as he picks up a fondue fork. I spear a marshmallow and dip it into the pot of dark chocolate between us. As I begin to lift it out, I feel a gentle pressure on my fork impeding the motion. I start to protest until I see the mischievous look on Matthew's face. He's nudging my marsh-mallow with the strawberry he's just covered in chocolate.

"My strawberry is getting it on with your marshmallow," he taunts quietly as he presses the berry against the white confec-tion, smearing chocolate all over it as I giggle. He re-dips his strawberry and lifts it over the marshmallow, drizzling choco-late down onto it in a steady stream. "It's coming all over her face," he whispers with a grin.

At that I laugh out loud. At the same time, I feel the tiny, unexpected jolt of electricity from the depths of my belly to my clit. I watch as Matthew exerts the tiniest bit of force to trap my fork with his, the submission of my utensil solidified with the clink of metal and my inability to extract it from beneath his.

I bite my lip. As he slides his fork down mine like a dominant sword, I remind myself that it's just fondue—there's no reason to get so excited. But as Matthew runs his drenched strawberry up the side of my marshmallow with painstaking slowness, I raise my eyes to his and see that his look is exactly what it is when he's fucking me, when he's holding me down and whis-pering how much he loves me as he slams his cock into me with a force much like that which he uses now to pin my hapless marshmallow against the molten liquid between us.

My breath has changed; I am right on the line between embarrassed and not giving a shit that the dessert course in a fancy restaurant has turned me on so much I want to rip my clothes off for him right there in our booth.

Matthew's eyes gleam as his lips lift in the faintest of grins. He knows exactly what he's doing.

When he finally relinquishes it, my fondue fork slithers from under his. The marshmallow is completely covered with melted dark chocolate. I lift it from the pot and bring to my mouth. Just before it reaches my lips, I pause. Chocolate drips, and I almost wince as the hot liquid lands on the cleavage my formal corset has positioned into ample view.

Matthew's eyes follow the dark stream. My tongue barely teases out between my lips, just in case it hasn't occurred to him to imagine what he wants to do with the chocolate now sliding down my skin. I hold his gaze until I feel the heat near my corset, then break eye contact and innocently reach for my napkin, obliterating this tiny impetus for my husband's latest fantasy.

"Check please," Matthew requests politely as our server wanders by.

I grin. "What time is it, darling?"

"Eleven fifteen." The lust in his eyes feels like it is physically crossing the expanse between us, reaching into me and feeding the fire burning in my core. "Let's go."

Matthew doesn't make the turn that would take us home—the most reliable place to carry out our tradition.

"Where are we going?"

He chuckles softly. "Where would you like to go?"

"Somewhere it would be appropriate for me to rip this corset open and start breathing again." My laugh is breathless—admittedly, there is more than one reason I'm ready to get out of my clothes.

"That's what I had in mind."

He follows the highway out past the city limits, into the land of expansive woods we often hike and picnic in—during the day. They appear deserted at this hour, and Matthew turns down a dirt road that dead-ends into a small parking lot.

Wishing I could physically shove the steering wheel out of the way, I ignore it and climb on top of him before he can even move. His hands are quick to engulf me as I grind myself against him.

With surprising deftness, he unhooks the corset constraining my flesh and my breasts spill out, inches from his face.

I gasp at the firmness of his lips and teeth on my nipple. Fumbling to find his zipper, I yank his pants open and pull out his cock. With a little maneuvering, my long skirt fans out around me, covering us both like a tablecloth as the delicate skin of my freshly shaved vulva touches the heat of his erection.

Matthew grabs me and tries to shove me onto his hard cock, and my breath catches. His urgency, the degree to which he wants me—hard, fast, now—never fails to turn me on. I see him glance at the clock, and I turn to follow his gaze over my shoulder. 11:47.

His grin meets mine as I turn back to him, and he reaches to open the door. The silent night air greets us as Matthew helps me off his lap and out of the car, following me and guiding me up to the hood. Before I can speak, he hoists me onto the warm metal, spreading my legs and pushing into me with a need that makes me cry out. I'm not worried about anyone hearing us. We're pretty far from civilization.

Matthew grabs my shoulders as his cock slams in and out of me, and my body goes limp as I take him as deep as I know how, feeling like I'm floating despite the hard metal beneath me that allows my body to push back and meet his.

I feel his thumb on my clit. My eyes open. Matthew has paused, his breathing heavy as he looks down at me, circling my clitoris with a gentleness that is astonishing given the urgency I can feel pounding through both of us.

It is the look in his eyes that makes me come, the combination of savage lust and conscious adoration that lights up the explosion in me and lets loose the unabashed scream that shoots from my throat. I grab him as I finish, loving him with everything I am as I pull his body down hard onto mine. His carnal rhythm returns, and I feel him come inside me, lifting his head so that he's looking in my eyes as he empties himself, his fingers curling around my hair and pulling tight.

There is no sound but our breath as our bodies recover, heartbeats slowing until they are part of the night, until the silence becomes our own.

I turn my head to see the watch on Matthew's wrist, still tangled in my hair. He follows my gaze.

12:05.

My grin is involuntary.

"Year six successfully completed," my husband murmurs as he pushes himself to standing and reaches to help me up.

The first year it was coincidence. Our naked bodies happened to be entangled the moment the clock struck midnight—the exact moment my birthday ended and his began. We had only discovered the adjacency of our birthdays a few weeks prior, having only known each other a couple of months at the time.

"Happy birthday, baby," I whisper with a smile.

As soon as I am standing, Matthew's kiss threatens to engulf me again, pull me like a blissful anchor to the depths of arousal from which I've just surfaced. I feel a bit dizzy as we back apart.

"Thank you," he answers as our mouths separate.

We climb back into the car, and I fuss a bit with my corset, maneuvering it so it will cover me at least partially during the drive. Matthew turns the key and sets a hand on my thigh as we head home, our tradition intact.

SOLDIER BOY

Sommer Marsden

've been thinking about you." He whispered it against the back of my neck as I doled out tickets. He'd slipped into my booth undetected.

Jarrod had been gone two long months for training; I'd missed him so. My heart strained, a runaway beat, as I tried to stay calm.

"Thank you and enjoy your night. Thank you and enjoy your night..." I repeated it over and over again as I handed out tickets for the fair.

Jarrod pressed against me, his lips on the back of my neck, his breathing synced up with mine. I had to clear my throat to get the words out, "Sorry, last roll. I'll have to get more," I said softly, putting up the closed sign and shutting my window.

"You had to work tonight of all nights?" he asked, capturing my face in his hands. Kissing me like I was some fragile thing.

"I'm sorry, I'm sorry. God, how I missed you." I grabbed his hand and we slipped from the booth.

This was just a summer job before my last year of college began. If I lost it, I lost it. They could have the job. All I wanted was the man who'd left many weeks ago and taken a bit of my heart with him.

"Kiss me," I said, pulling him under the roller coaster. Above us the clackety old wooden thing groaned. The fair touted it as one of the oldest wooden coasters in use. Judging by what we heard, I wasn't sure they should be bragging.

Jarrod pushed me up against a support beam, big hands I loved so much worming up under my red-and-white-striped regulation tee. "As if you have to tell me that, Ashley-girl. Fuck, I missed you." His lips skated along my throat, down over my collarbone. His hips ground to mine even as the coaster shook us. I could feel his cock rub the split of my sex through my jeans. I could feel my insides going soft and warm for him.

Yes, I could live with losing this job. My soldier was home. Who knew for how long? He was home and they could have their rolls of yellow tickets and their concession stand shifts and their hours of cleanup patrol. And their eight bucks an hour. He was home and he was here.

I put my hand on his belt buckle, tugging him against me. His hands found my breasts, popped my bra cups down. He cupped me with big warm hands and when I let myself relax into his touch, he pinched me. The sensation speared through me swiftly.

Too many days to count had passed without his touch, and now within moments I was ready. I was willing. And tucked under the giant roller coaster, I was able.

"Back farther, come along, soldier boy," I said against his ear so he could hear me.

"I'd follow you anywhere, Ashley."

It made me blush because he meant it. Two years of dating,

separation when he went away, and the weight of life hadn't tamed what I felt for him. And I knew he felt the same.

I'd not only missed his caress and our intimacy, I'd missed it all. He was my best friend, and I feared where they'd station him now. The fear coiled in my gut, but I pushed it away. That was for later. Now was the time to feel his skin against mine.

I pushed my back to another ancient support beam and prayed that rickety old coaster would hold and not come down on us. What a way to go, death by sex and roller coaster.

I laughed and he grinned, his face barely visible in the murky light. "What's so funny?"

"Just praying there won't be a cave in."

"Ah..." His hands pushed under the tail of my shirt again, smoothing their way across my skin, his palms balmy and whispering where they touched me. "I don't see this old thing coming down anytime soon. But these...I think these might." He pushed at my shorts and I shimmied my hips to help him.

Then I was standing in the shade and dust in my bright pink panties.

"And these," Jarrod said, pushing those down, too. He knelt for a minute; lucky him, his camo would hide the dirt. His mouth pressed to me, tongue darting out to taste me. It was rushed and furtive. We were in a hurry. I felt it as surely as he did. There would be time for lingering later. So after a few stunning licks of that wet scorching tongue of his, I put my hand out for him to stand.

"More of that later," I said, my lips pressed to the small *V* of tanned skin above his uniform shirt. I wrestled his pants button and zipper, finally finding him, hot and hard, with my hand.

When I squeezed him he said, "God I've missed your hands on me. And your mouth." He touched my lips. "And everything else. Just the sound of you breathing was absent."

My heart crimped up and I shook my head because if I spoke, I'd cry. My heart had been so heavy with him gone. "Hush up now and come closer, soldier boy."

He pressed against me, his pants only down to midthigh, his cock sliding against my thigh. I hooked my leg up around his hip, parting my nether lips, opening my body for him with just that simple motion.

He groaned and then laughed, kissing my lips, my cheeks, my neck as he slid the tip of his cock through my moisture. I tilted my hips to force his movement. I wanted him in me. We could go slow later.

Jarrod surrendered to my movement, sliding into me with ease. We stilled for a moment, that heartbeat of time flash frozen under the rumble of the roller coaster and wrapped in the heat of the day.

And then we were moving. Me up to take him, him forward to fill me. A simple fluid dance of lovers well acquainted but still enticed by each other. I captured his lower lip between my teeth and bit gently so he groaned again. Fingers gripping the meat of my hips, he slammed against me, his pubic bone banging my clit deliciously so that when I tensed my internal muscles I came. A slow, supple sound slid out of me. It was more of a whimper than a moan. I remembered in that instant how my chest had ached with missing him.

"I'm home," he said, reading my mind. When I kissed the words away, he held my waist tight and thrust into me once more, filling me fully and then emptying into me with a groan.

"I know. I just missed you *so* much," I said, wiping away a tear that embarrassed me.

He wiped the other eye. Studied me. "California is my destination," he said, fishing in his pocket.

My heart dropped and I stooped to find my panties so I

could hide my face from him. California was so far away. Three thousand long and lonely miles. When I pulled my panties up I saw the small velvet box held by the man I'd missed so much I had physically hurt.

"So what do you say, Ashley-girl?" he asked, prying back the lid so I could see the ring inside. "Want to see California with me? I'm sure they have cloying heat and old roller coasters and most of all, they'll have me. I can't imagine going without you."

He kissed me without letting me answer, and finally after months that felt like forever, my heart was light.

ANNIVERSARY WRAPPINGS

Kathleen Tudor

Through, then over...shit! No, it's okay, now push the loop over the other loop... Two sticks, a whole lot of string (okay, yarn), and hours and hours of patiently torturing myself were about to come together in one final, amazing, wonderful finished product.

"Yes!" I pulled the last loop of yarn off of the knitting needle and held up the finished scarf. It was a bit uneven, but it was my first finished knitting project and I was so ready to be done with it. All I had left was to sew the ends in, and I was set.

Well, James was set. I'd only been dating him for a couple of weeks when my best friend Sherry decided to teach me to knit, and I figured a scarf for him would make a wonderful first project. Today was our one-year anniversary, and I was finally finished with his gift.

It made me a little misty to think of how the ups and downs of our first year together paralleled my waxing and waning interest in the project. There were times I never wanted to see another knitting needle again, or anything that shade of blue, but eventually I always picked it up again, determined to finish what I had started. And over that same period, James and I had developed something special, not because we never fought or never made mistakes, but because we were able to become a better couple by working through the problems that we encountered.

I started to wrap the scarf up in a bit of tissue paper for him, but then I had a better idea.

The cashmere merino blend was soft and erotic against my skin whenever I'd wrapped it around my neck to test the length. I pulled off my clothes, discarding the sweet outfit I'd chosen for our anniversary dinner, and tried to "put on" the scarf, instead. I wrapped it half a dozen ways, but I eventually had to settle for tying it around my breasts so that the tails hung over my light brown pubic curls.

I giggled as I waited for him to arrive with our takeout, and my heart sped when I heard his tap at the door. Bouncing with eagerness, I stood behind the door as I opened it to keep myself out of view of the hall, and then shut it behind him, giving him a perfect view of my scantily wrapped self. He moved straight past me, unnoticing as he went to unpack the boxes of Thai goodies.

It would have been easy to be frustrated, but I had come to know James as a single-minded man. It was only a matter of time before...yes, there it was. He glanced up, probably wondering why I wasn't right at his elbow to steal the first bite of my favorite spicy chicken, and froze as soon as his eyes locked on me.

His mouth hung slightly open as if he'd been about to speak, and his eyes were wide, taking me in.

"I finished your scarf," I told him, giving a little bounce on my heels. My breasts jiggled as I moved, and the tails of the scarf danced merrily in front of my pussy.

He opened his mouth, closed it again, and then smiled. "I see that. I should probably try it on, then, shouldn't I?"

A shiver went through me from head to toe as he moved toward me. Then he untied the knot at my breasts and pulled it away from me, draping it around his own neck as he stepped back.

"What do you think?" he asked.

I laughed but couldn't think of a thing to say. Fortunately James was quicker. He stepped close to me again, and brushed his knuckles over my erect nipples. The strange naughtiness of being naked while he was clothed was making me hot and cold with arousal, and my body was responding with fierce heat between my legs and the pebbling of my nipples.

"Poor thing," he said, "you look cold! Maybe you need the scarf more than I do."

I opened my mouth to protest, and he pressed the scarf across my lips, sealing in whatever I might have said. He laughed as he wrapped it around my head and tied it with a knot, leaving me mute and blind, my hearing strangely muffled by the soft fabric. I jumped when he sucked one hard nipple into his mouth. His tongue teased over it, and we both moaned as he sucked hard.

Then he switched to my other breast and I lifted my hands to grab fistfuls of his hair, sighing in pleasure as I felt the heat of his mouth on my skin. His hands roamed over my back and hips, then he shifted and grabbed me and I felt myself lifted into the air. After a disorienting but short trip, he tossed me through the air and I squeaked into the scarf a second before I bounced onto the bed.

His clothes rustled and I heard his belt hit the ground then felt the sensation of the bed dipping beneath me. His hands were on me again, teasing across my breasts and then traipsing over my belly with featherlight touches that tormented and aroused. I relaxed and opened to him, and then nearly jumped out of my skin when I felt the heat of his mouth again, this time on my clit. He laughed and I writhed, my legs dropping open for him as he sucked my clit into his mouth.

Something about not being able to see him made the sensations more intense as he flicked his tongue over that sensitive nub or reached up to pinch my nipple or stroke gentle fingers along my collarbone. I could smell his earthy shampoo almost as if my face were buried in his soft hair, and hear every wet sucking sound as he teased me skillfully with his lips and tongue. And then I felt his fingers probe at my opening, and I moaned, soft and low.

With his fingers added to the dance, it was only seconds before he had me panting and thrashing. I pulled the scarf away and light burst in my vision, glorious and beautiful and powerful as I came. I cried out, clutching the soft, knitted fabric as my body trembled and quivered with pleasure beneath his onslaught.

He laughed again and kissed me, and I tasted the sweet tang of my own arousal on his lips and tongue. I thought he would enter me then, but he pushed my hands up over my head with one hand and straddled my stomach, smiling down at me.

"I like your present," he said, and gently unwound it from around my throat before bringing it up and wrapping it around my wrists.

"I like it too," I said, and moaned as he wrapped the scarf around the headboard and pulled it tight. My arms were stretched above my head in a sensation that was both completely foreign and somehow totally natural and incredibly sexy. I was under his power, and though I could probably have worked my hands free from their knots, it didn't even occur to me to try.

James eased back and stood, his gaze traveling from my bound hands down my body and back up again, and his erection seemed to throb and swell as he examined me. "Fuck, baby, every time I wear that scarf I'm going to think of you modeling it for me, just like this." He reached down and idly stroked his cock as if that thought made it impossible to resist, and I whimpered, wanting him.

"Fuck me," I whispered, and he moved over me with a groan and thrust inside. I moaned and moved to wrap my arms around him and maybe to dig my nails into his back to encourage him to move. The scarf pulled tight and held my arms above my head, and I moaned again, louder, as the reality of being bound sent a surge of heat through my body, straight to my pussy.

James smiled and eased back for a slow, lazy stroke, his grin getting bigger every second as he realized that he would get the long, slow fuck he loved rather than the frenzied pace I usually drove him to. "Fuck me!" I cried, trying to use my hips to drive him deeper.

"Oh, I will," he whispered back. "Just think of this as slow motion."

He took over an hour, stroking with slow patience, driving me half-mad with arousal, and I don't remember most of it. When I finally came, it was with atomic force, screaming and thrashing against my gentle bonds as my body surrendered to the most intense orgasm I could imagine.

The next thing I knew, I was snuggled in James's arms, his new scarf wrapped once around his neck. He grinned at my dazed expression. "I think our dinner is cold."

BECAUSE HE KNOWS HER SO WELL

Saskia Walker

Carrie's blood pumped, excess adrenaline keeping her edgy and alert. She zipped up her jacket, secured her backpack and set off down the dark London street at a jog. Anyone who saw her would have assumed she was on her way to start an early shift. She wasn't. Carrie had been at work for the past twelve hours, nursing on the front line in the emergency department. It had been a hell of a shift, which meant she was even more wired and edgy than usual. The twenty-minute jog home sometimes helped to work the adrenaline out of her system, but she had the feeling it wouldn't cut it today. She pushed herself, huffing in the cold winter air as she pounded the empty streets toward the rented flat they called home. Jackson would be asleep and she didn't want to wake him by pacing around the flat, trying to work off her day.

When she got to the building she took the stairs then stopped outside their door, key fob in her gloved hand. Her body ached to be naked and sliding in alongside Jackson in bed, but she wasn't sleepy. Jackson would be warm and supine, and he'd kiss her lazily as he hugged her in against him, his cock at half-mast in his semiwaking state. The thought of it arrested her completely, redirecting that excess adrenaline to her sex drive. Moaning beneath her breath, she rued this badly timed life they were leading. She'd signed up for too many night shifts recently. Saving their pennies for an important house purchase meant that sacrifices were being made, maybe too many.

Quietly, Carrie let herself into their rented home. When the door closed behind her, she walked through the dark hallway. It was warm, and the distant whir of the boiler let her know that Jackson had put the timer on so the heating would be on when she got home.

She paused when a feeling of uncertainty crept over her. She was about to turn and look over her shoulder, when she was grabbed from behind.

Her heart jolted, then she felt Jackson's hot, familiar kiss on the side of her neck.

His arms locked around her, drawing her in against him.

Gasping, she covered his bare hand with her gloved hands. "You should be in bed."

"How can I sleep when I know you're about to arrive and you're bound to be horny?" He moved his hands inside her thermal jacket to stroke her breasts though her top.

Carrie caught her bottom lip between her teeth, her adrenaline level only rising. Was it wise to fool around though? At midday they were due at the solicitor's to sign papers, important papers. "Jackson, we've got a busy day ahead."

"Yes, we commit to our first proper home, the one we chose and bought together." He kissed her behind her ear, and his whispered words made her ache for him. "But you always do say a solid two hours serves you better than five hours' restless sleep. So, I'm going to make sure you're not restless."

Bending slightly at the waist, she leaned into him, enjoying the hard line of his body against her back. "Mmm, that sounds so good."

"Oh no you don't. That's not what I had in mind." He kissed her earlobe. "Well, not right away." Turning her to face him, he caged her against the wall with his hands either side of her head then kissed her, long and slow.

Carrie tugged off her gloves, casting them to the floor, and ran her hands over his body. He was completely naked, his skin warm from sleep. When her fingers wrapped around his rising cock, he thrust his tongue into her mouth and closed right up against her, his erection squashed against her belly through her clothing.

She pressed her fingers demandingly into the firm muscle of his gorgeous ass. "Please, Jackson. I'm so turned on."

"Patience, my love." He took her hand and led her to the bathroom. Switching on the shower faucet, he indicated she should strip.

She was trembling with need by the time she was naked.

When she got into the shower he joined her.

Carrie stood with her shoulders under the stream of hot water and stared at him, loving the way he looked, from his closely shorn hair to his lean chest, narrow hips and fit, cyclist's thighs. Was he really hers? Were they really buying a home together? It felt like a huge commitment.

"I'm going to take my time with this," he announced.

"Tease."

He smiled and lathered her breasts and abdomen, his hands moving in a slow rhythm over her body. She had to grasp his shoulder to hold steady when he moved lower and rubbed back and forth over her pussy, sparking her clit. She was desperate to be taken roughly and pushed to climax.

He kissed her face while the water rinsed them both off, then toweled her off and nodded his head toward the bedroom.

Carrie tried not to race ahead. She got onto the bed while she watched him cross the room to her side. His fist locked around the base of his cock and he stroked it up and down in a lazy movement. It looked so hot she reached out and grabbed for him.

He shifted, escaping her reach. "How much do you want it?"

"Jackson!"

He strolled around the bed and lay down next to her, crossing his hands behind his head. "I just wondered."

Carrie stared at his cock, arching provocatively from his hips, long and hard and rigid. She wanted him so badly that she would have got down on her hands and knees and begged him to fuck her.

He grinned at her.

She saw it and laughed softly, lifting her eyebrows at him accusingly. "You bastard!"

He'd got her to a fever pitch, and now he was challenging her to climb on top. Her face flamed. Usually it took a couple of glasses of wine to get rid of her self-consciousness for that particular position, but he liked to tease her about it.

Again he stroked his erection, inviting her to mount it.

She clenched, need driving her—the need to burn them back together after the difficult hours apart, the need to demonstrate their love in physical terms. With her bottom lip captured between her teeth, she straddled him. Hands trembling with need, she drew his cock to her and pressed it to her damp flesh. As her body took him in, she closed her eyes, relishing the intense pressure of his cock thrusting up inside her, filling her as she sank down onto him.

Whispering words of encouragement, Jackson praised her when she began to rock back and forth. "You look gorgeous, you shameless hussy."

"Bastard!" But it felt so good that she didn't really care about how she looked anymore. Instead, she gripped his shoulders and rode him with determination.

Jackson locked his hands on her hips, holding her to him when she grew frantic, the imminence of climax making her wild and uninhibited.

"Oh yes, I'm right there for you, lover. I've been longing for you to get home to me."

That tipped her over the edge and she worked on him fast and furious, until her hips bucked and she came, her core clenching rhythmically on his cock.

Jackson cursed under his breath and arched against the bed, the muscles in his neck cording as he poured himself into her.

Wilting over him, she sighed with relief.

Rolling her onto her back, he kissed her as he withdrew.

She was almost ready for sleep but blinked up at him. He had something to say, she could tell. "What?"

"How well do I know you?"

She smiled. He'd let her loose again, and it was just what she'd needed. "It was a tough night on the ward."

"I know. So…"

"You know me very well."

"Well enough to sign these papers together?"

Carrie ran her fingers over his head and nodded. She hadn't realized he knew she was worried about that.

"I know you better than you think." He smiled, one corner of his mouth lifting.

Tangling her hands together around the back of his neck she laughed softly and nodded. "You certainly do."

He tapped his chest with one finger, and she rolled in against him as he lay down, resting her head in her favorite place as she happily snuggled in her lover's arms. It felt good, listening to his heartbeat as she drifted into sleep. It felt right to Carrie, and Jackson held her tightly to him because he knew that.

CONTROL

A. J. Lyle

Bailey's stomach clenched with anticipation. Standing beside the king-size bed, completely naked in the center of their honeymoon suite, she could admit that the fear of saying, "I do," at the altar didn't come close to the anxiety she felt at that moment, waiting for her husband.

She ran her fingers through her short red hair. Control was something she retained at all times, and yet, somehow, Asher had a way of making her want to feel powerless just for him. His sexy-as-hell grin and beseeching eyes had been her downfall from the very beginning.

Oh, but what a grand fall it had been.

The bathroom door clicked open behind her and she froze. A shot of apprehension surged, and her skin tingled.

"Look at me."

His deep voice slid over and around her, and a chill crept up the back of her neck. She turned and drank in the sight of his muscular body, heat igniting in the depths of her abdomen.

Faded blue jeans hung on his tight frame, sagging just low enough to tease, and a black leather belt was draped over his shoulder. Chocolate-brown eyes pierced into hers. The sheer power radiating from them sent her back a step.

"Ash, what—"

Asher stalked forward, one slow step at a time, his eyes smoldering and a small smile playing at the corners of his full lips. "Do you trust me?"

Bailey frowned. There was no doubt in her mind. "Of course, but—"

He stroked the leather belt slowly, waiting to make sure he had her attention. Closing the few feet between them, he pulled her hips hard against him. His erection rubbed against her, and she stifled a groan. Asher's dark eyes glittered with sensual promise.

"It's a simple question, babe. Yes or no?"

"Yes," she breathed.

"I'm going to make you scream my name over and over, Mrs. Asher Thomas, and I don't want you saying you can't handle the intensity of your pleasure."

Bailey's breath caught and she shook her head. "I can't—"

Brushing his lips over hers, he whispered, "You can."

Shivers shot down her back as he trailed his tongue down her throat and across her shoulder.

"What's...the belt for?" she whispered, her voice unsteady.

He chuckled, a deep, throaty sound. "You won't know unless you trust me." He grasped her hair at the back of her neck and pulled lightly. "I want control tonight, lover. Complete...and utter...control."

Bailey let her head fall back in his grip, losing herself in the heat of his lips moving up her neck to her earlobe. Hot breath assaulted her, and he tugged her hair again. She sucked in a sharp breath, reveling in the rush of being dominated by her husband. *Husband.* Oh, how she loved the sound of that.

"I trust you."

Asher stepped back and released her, slipping the belt from his shoulder. His lips spread in a wide, it-feels-like-Christmas grin for a second, but then he licked his lips and all that remained was a wicked little smile that made her heart flip-flop.

"Lie on your stomach on the bed," he commanded. "Put your hands behind your head. Hurry."

His commanding tone crept through her defenses and wakened a desire to submit that she'd never felt before. This was a side of him she'd never seen. A nervous twitter worked up her spine, but she moved her hands into place. "I'm a little scared."

The bed shifted with his body weight as he climbed up behind her. He trailed his fingertips up her spine. "You should be. Rule one: obey without question."

Asher pushed her legs apart and rubbed his palm along her slit. She gasped. Dipping his finger into her juices and rubbing her tight entrance in a punishing circle, he continued, "Rule two: obey as fast as you can."

He reached under her stomach and lifted her hips up off the bed, settling her on her knees. "Hold them there."

Bailey heard the belt snap behind her, and she turned to look at him. Her heartbeat thundered in her ears. "What are you going to do?"

Asher's dark brows shot up. "Did you question me?" He shook his head and clicked his tongue. "You naughty, naughty girl."

She bit her bottom lip to keep from whimpering as his hand once again stroked her, two fingers slipping into her with ease. Her sheath tightened around him. He knew just where and how to touch to drive her crazy with need.

"You're so hot and wet. Mmm...do you like that?"

"Yes," she breathed.

She closed her eyes, absorbing the soft sensation, when all of a sudden a bolt of molten heat connected with her left asscheek. Her eyes shot open and she yelped, but before she could respond, the belt landed with a slap against the other cheek. He twisted his fingers inside her, brushing against her G-spot with every thrust. Again and again the belt slapped down, never in the same spot twice. The temporary sting of the impact merged into a delicious burning, like the embers of a fire that ever so slowly worked their way down her legs and up the small of her back.

And through it all, came the soft pleasure of his ministrations within her pulsing sheath. The belt snapped against her, lower this time. The vibrations shot straight to her core.

"And that?"

Bailey's breath came faster. "Y...yes."

"Rule three: never hesitate." His deep voice reverberated through her, and the belt once again bit into her flesh. Holding her hips steady was almost too much to remember while losing herself in the rhythm of his exquisite torture.

He stopped abruptly, just short of her orgasm, and she writhed with need. A second later his hands gripped hers. He slid the belt around them, secured them behind her head, and tugged on the loose end, lifting her front and causing her to strain to keep her hips steady. She listened in anticipation as his jeans slid down to free his hard shaft.

"You want this?" he asked, his voice low and husky.

"Oh, yes."

He positioned himself between her legs again, but this time, it was the warmth of his cock that prodded her entrance. "What do you want, lover?"

"You, Asher."

"Tell me how."

Bailey took a deep breath. He knew how hard it was for her to talk dirty and she vowed to make him pay for it later. "I want you inside me."

She felt the tip of his cock push into her, but then he pulled back out. "Sorry, lover. Not good enough."

Bailey swallowed past the anxiety building in her throat. She knew how he liked it. "I...want..."

Asher circled her opening with his tip. "Yes?"

"I want you to fuck me with your hard cock."

"Oh fuck, yes."

He pushed in, hard, stretching her. She gasped at the sudden invasion. "Ash, wait, I..."

He pulled out right to the tip and tugged on the belt, reminding her that she was at his mercy. "You want to be punished, don't you, dirty girl?"

He plunged into her again, his hand landing hard on her ass and sending a jolt of fire to ignite in her core. Asher withdrew yet again, and she whimpered, her orgasm already building deep inside her belly.

"Don't you?" he persisted.

"Y—yes," she gasped.

His tongue clicked in response and he plunged again. "Just can't listen." With a small smile, he continued, "Rule four: you orgasm only when I tell you to."

Bailey shuddered as he stroked in and out, hard and fast. How the hell was she supposed to stop it?

Whether he willed it to or not, her inner core coiled tight, and before she could stop herself, she was flying high on the throes of her fulfillment. He rode her until she cried out, allowing her to feel the climax before pulling out and flipping her over beneath him.

He hovered above her, his eyes hard and unrelenting. "You've broken every rule, babe," he whispered.

Still quivering from her orgasm, she met his challenging stare with her own. "I know."

Asher's lips twitched with amusement. "I see. Well, there's only one way to train a woman like you."

Bailey yelped at the pressure of his fingers closing tight around her nipple.

"Oh?" she breathed.

"Lots and lots of practice."

He leaned down and caught her other nipple between his teeth, flicking it lightly with his tongue before finally pulling it into his mouth.

"Lots, meaning...?" she asked breathlessly.

Asher grinned against her skin. "The rest of our lives, babe."

UNSNUBBED

Jeremy Edwards

The jumble of shirts, maps, bras, panties and professional journals on my hotel room bed was a microcosm of my life. It was remarkable how quickly a sleek, shiny business-pleasure trip came to replicate the tangled, mundane mess of one's general existence—and how quickly excitement-charged luggage began its metamorphosis into humdrum laundry.

I'd arrived only one day early—yesterday—to tour favorite old college haunts; and yet looking at the bed now, one would think it was the location of a particularly fruitful archaeological dig that had unearthed the relics of a particularly untidy civilization.

The clothing-heaped bed reminded me of campus parties— winter parties, in which lovers of the moment could invariably be found entwined among an orgy of overcoats on someone's mattress. The kinds of parties I'd never accepted Benjamin's invitations to attend.

The event at the center of this visit was a bit of a jumble

itself, half reunion and half conference. The celebrated archae-ological theorist who ran the program I'd graduated from—a special five-year undergrad track culminating in a master's—thought it would be both valuable and enjoyable to have his alums converge for a long weekend, on the occasion of the proj-ect's twenty-fifth anniversary. "The subdisciplines in our field take us in widely different directions," Professor Burnell's letter had noted. "In the summer of 2000, I would like to see us come together, not only as alumni but as scholars, to share our experi-ences and insights."

It had always been a small program, and with a quarter-century spread defining the eligible population, the final list of attendees included exactly one person I knew: Benjamin. A twinge of guilt had gone through me when I saw his name.

It wasn't that I had an aversion to Ben in our college days. In fact, I thought he was quite cute. But I was a late bloomer, sexually speaking, and developing bedroom relationships with guys—even cute guys who kept inviting me to parties—just wasn't a priority.

And so Ben would invite me out, and I would say no, and when the pattern became unmistakably clear, he stopped asking. I was fine with all that—I didn't feel guilty about having said no when I wasn't motivated to say yes. But what I wasn't at all fine with, looking back, was the fact that I'd snubbed him for his music-listening preferences.

Sadly, I was a little too cool with my punk-or-nothing music tastes, and when I learned Ben favored progressive rock, I began ridiculing him for this at every opportunity. I didn't mean to be cruel; in the impossibly dogmatic environment of 1980s college-radio culture, it was basically a knee-jerk reaction. But, regret-tably, it became the only type of discussion I would bother to have with him—if one person snickering in condescension while the other says nothing can be called a discussion. What made it worse was this abuse had started the semester *after* he'd given up asking me on dates. Talk about adding insult to injury, I thought ruefully now.

In the self-induced claustrophobia of a messy hotel room, I stood wondering: was it too late to *un*snub Benjamin? We were in our midthirties. Would Ben give a damn one way or another what that snotty classmate of his said or did at a two-day reunion?

Maybe not. But the snotty classmate gave a damn.

I sat awkwardly on the only available corner of the bed to analyze my feelings, which seemed to go deeper than mere repentance for immature behavior. The soul-searching was a mental exercise…but the answer came in a very physical form, as my legs spread wider over the mattress corner and my hand came to rest at the front of my cotton panties: thinking about Benjamin was acutely turning me on. The state of arousal I'd let bubble under the surface all day, lazily content in the knowledge that there was another orgasm somewhere in my immediate future, had found a compelling focus—and, having found it, demanded my urgent attention.

He wasn't hard to spot at cocktail hour, though his neat hair and well-tailored young professor ensemble were new to me, and his face had acquired a few handsome lines. It was a face—thoughtful and gentle, with a thin but expressive mouth—that I remembered better than I'd realized.

Our eyes met, and I blushed with the memory of my frantic fingers twisting my clitoris an hour earlier—and the consciousness that my unscheduled late-afternoon solo sex had pushed me across the International Date Line, laundrywise. In other words, thanks to a reverie involving the very man walking toward me, I was currently inhabiting tomorrow's underwear.

"Hi, Allie!"

He seemed genuinely glad to see me. I sighed guiltily before returning his smile.

"Hello, Benjamin."

We approached for a light-hug, cheek-graze.

When we parted, I stole another eyeful of his face, while his scent—like espresso cut with cumin—still lingered. "Cute" simply didn't do justice to the dashing look Benjamin had grown into. If I'd been hot for his memory upstairs, I was now officially horny for his present incarnation. Horny...but guilt ridden.

"Can I get you a drink?" he offered. "Burnell has provided us with an amazing Malbec. I swear, this wine has so much personality it would stand up straight even without a glass."

I laughed, with surprise as well as delight. I'd forgotten that Ben was *funny*, on top of everything else.

He touched my arm to direct me to the drinks table; I shuddered with a paradoxical mixture of abandon and self-consciousness when I realized I'd dampened my fresh panties in response. I determined that I had to get the unsnubbing over with—or cream myself trying. After all, what was the point of melting in my underwear for Benjamin if I was too preoccupied with ancient guilt to fully enjoy it?

"Hey, this is my chance to finally apologize to you," I said, after he'd handed me my wine.

"Apologize? What for?"

"You know. For back then."

He glanced over his shoulder, as if I'd said, "back *there*"—though I knew he'd heard me correctly. God, he was adorable.

"Huh? What happened 'back then'?"

"I sort of snubbed you," I said with a wince.

"You did?"

I nodded sheepishly.

He laughed. "You must not have done it very effectively, then, because I don't believe I ever got the message."

He took a sip of wine and made a sour, Malbec-unrelated face. "Damn, I must have been a pain, asking you out time after time."

"No, you were fine," I said earnestly. "But don't you remember my mocking you for your taste in music?"

"I honestly don't." He grinned. "All I remember is how much I liked you."

And despite all my insecurities, I believed him—believed that Ben had continued to like me through all my obnoxiousness... that he'd liked me enough to not even *notice* I was obnoxious.

While the words "how much I liked you" reverberated in my tingling ears, I reflected for a moment on Benjamin's unself-conscious generosity, and I thought I might start to cry. Then I felt the sudden bliss of my mood unburdening, and I found myself chuckling with relief. The man had put me completely at ease.

"And here I was all set to unsnub you."

"Well, don't let me stop you," Ben replied. "I'd love to be unsnubbed—it sounds like fun."

I looked into Ben's eyes. He was here. He was beautiful, kind, and utterly delicious. He was, quite possibly, everything I'd ever wanted in a long-term lover.

And he would certainly not proposition me, having so recently apologized for being "a pain." But that didn't mean I couldn't proposition *him*, I told myself decisively.

"Unsnubbing," I said slowly, "is best done upstairs."

If my personal effects had resembled a dig site on the bed, they became a hailstorm of literature and underclothes as I swept them to the floor. But I didn't apologize for the disorder. If anything, I felt confident and wise as I gave the clutter the heave-ho, as if clearing the decks for a session of unrestrained gratification had symbolic significance.

Life, I reflected again, was a matter of priorities—and right now, my top priority was getting Benjamin's sensitive lips between my legs.

There's nothing like having an eager, devoted mouth on your pussy to make you feel that all your past rudeness has truly been forgiven, every instance of your pettiness and insensitivity forgotten. As Ben ate me out, I was squirming almost as much from the caress of emotional redemption as I was from the sizzles and shocks of pleasure being delivered to my moist and hungry sex.

Almost. Because when I screamed and pounded my fists on the mattress, *that* was pure physical pleasure.

"And now, Allie," Ben purred, "I'd like to see us come together...not only as alumni..."

A renowned scholar like Professor Burnell is always getting quoted, you see.

DESIGNATED DRIVER

Heidi Champa

I sat watching him fumble with the keys, trying in vain to start the car. All he had managed to do was scratch the starter. His overfilled key chain rattled in the dark, before dropping to the floor. He picked it up, only to fail again in his attempt to get our car started. He gave up and slumped back in his seat.

"You'll have to drive, Becca. I can't."

"What makes you think I can?"

He looked at me, annoyed. "You're not as drunk as me."

"But, I'm still drunk, Steve."

He sighed and pulled the keys from the ignition, tossing them back and forth between his hands. Suddenly, he threw the keys into the backseat where they landed with a thud on the leather.

"Well, I guess we'll have to kill some time before we go home."

"We don't have time to kill. The babysitter is expecting us in half an hour."

"I guess we shouldn't have ordered that second bottle of wine."

"Maybe not."

He tapped the steering wheel while I rummaged through my purse to find my phone.

"What are you doing?"

"Well, if we can't drive, we need a cab."

He took my phone from my hand before I could stop him, tossing it into the backseat as well.

"Why did you do that?"

"I don't want to take a cab."

"Then how do you propose we get home? We're grown-ups for god's sake. We can't risk driving drunk."

"That's why I suggested waiting a bit before we go."

"And, what are we supposed to do? Just sit here in the car and stare out the windshield."

"I'm sure if we put our heads together we could think of something to pass some time."

"We can't."

"Sure we can. We've been a little late coming home from dinner before. Stacy can handle an extra hour watching our satellite TV."

"So, then what are we going to do?"

"I have an idea, Becca."

He pushed his bucket seat all the way back and slouched down in it. When his hand settled over his crotch, I could tell that he was starting to get hard.

"Really, Steve? You want to have sex in the car?"

"Why not? No one can see us back here. Besides, it's been a while since we've done anything adventurous."

"You call this an adventure? Hell, it's more like nostalgia."

"Call it whatever you want. But, you look hot tonight. And I want you. Right here, right now."

"Seriously?"

"Absolutely. Now get over here."

He pulled me to him, our lips meeting over the console. Steve wasted no time taking my hand and putting it to his belt. I couldn't help but smile against his lips as I undid the leather and popped the button of his pants through the hole with one hand.

"Damn, you always were good at that, Becca."

"Lots of practice."

Once I had his zipper down, I reached inside his boxers and felt the warmth of his hard cock.

"You're really sure about this?"

"Come on. You can't leave me hanging. It's been so long since I've felt your mouth on me."

"It hasn't been that long."

"Can we argue about this later? Right now, I have other things on my mind."

Giving a quick look around until I was satisfied the parking lot was deserted, I dropped my head and took him into my mouth. He gasped above me, squirming as I ran my tongue up and down the underside of his shaft. Focusing all my attention on the swollen tip, I laved the velvet softness until he urged me to take him deeper by putting his hand through my hair. I obliged him, doing all the things I knew he liked, until he groaned with delight.

"Oh god, Becca. That feels amazing."

Soon, his fingers were groping my nipples through my shirt, teasing me through the thin silky fabric. Before I could do anything else, he tugged at the back of my blouse until my back was exposed and unhooked my bra. I stopped sucking him and looked up from his lap.

"Oops, sorry."

"I don't think you're sorry at all."

"You're right, I'm not."

"What's gotten into you tonight?"

"Must be all that wine."

Without warning, he zipped up and threw open the car door and stepped out into the night. As the sound of the slam still echoed, he reappeared in the backseat, undoing his pants as he pulled the back door closed. Tossing my phone and the keys onto the driver's seat he made himself more than comfortable. He smirked at me and I had to smile back.

"Well, are you going to join me or what?"

"Okay."

Extracting my bra from underneath my shirt, I tossed it onto the floor next to my purse. Once that was done, I straightened myself up as best I could and got out of the car, quickly rejoining Steve in the backseat. Everything looked different. I realized I had never been in the backseat of my own car. My thoughts were diverted back to Steve when he kissed me, slipping a hand under my skirt to caress my thigh.

"Now, where were we?"

The cheesy line, along with the waggle of his eyebrows, had me giggling. But the laughter died when I watched him stroke his cock back to life. I leaned over and took him into my mouth.

"Oh, right. Now I remember what we were doing."

His words came out in a strained whisper as I worked his cock in and out of my mouth, wrapping my fingers firmly around the base. It didn't take long for him to start losing his composure, and I could tell he was struggling to keep from coming. All his telltale signs were on display, but I was so wrapped up in the way he felt in my mouth that I didn't want to stop. Finally, after another long, slow slide of my tongue over and around his dick, I moved away from him.

He groaned as I sat up, but his distress quickly turned to a smile as I slid my panties out from under my skirt and tossed them forward to join my bra. I tried to move with grace and sensuality, but as usual, it didn't quite work out like I planned. As I tried to straddle him, I managed to hit my head on the ceiling.

"Careful, Becca. I don't want you knocking yourself out before I make you come."

He reached up, rubbing my scalp as he slid inside me, just the tip of his hard cock invading me. He rocked me forward with his hips, pressing a finger against my clit. I opened my blouse and he wasted no time before wrapping his soft lips around one of my nipples and licking it to a stiff peak. First one, then the other until I was the one panting and moaning. He was still just inside me an inch, his restraint remarkable. He sat back and looked up at me, his dark eyes barely visible in the dim light.

"I have to tell you something, Becca."

"What?"

"I'm not that drunk. I just wanted to fuck you."

He grinned up at me as I sank down on his cock with a sigh. God, he felt so good. So perfect. Just like always. I kissed him, moving my mouth around to his ear so he could hear me whisper.

"I'm not drunk either, Steve."

FRIEND OF THE COURT

Kelly Rand

It was after seven. Custodians had turned off some of the office lights and a vacuum cleaner hummed down the hall. Koryn's phone blinked with an unchecked voice mail message. Under the desk, she'd kicked off her high heels. Her lower back ached from sitting all day.

But she stayed late because Craig was staying late.

His office nameplate read CRAIG MALCOLM, CRIMINAL DEFENSE ATTORNEY, and Koryn's skin crawled when she heard even snippets of conversations about his cases. Husbands who beat their wives to death. Men caught with hard drives full of material Koryn could hardly imagine, let alone examine as evidence. She imagined that was why his jaw seemed so stiff and his blue eyes so hard. He had short blond hair, a closet full of Armani suits and a runner's body. And he was older than her. A lot older.

Koryn was twenty-three. Craig had turned thirty-seven earlier that week, a fact he only acknowledged after she sent him a text message asking if he wanted to have dinner. They always had dinner in his office, never outside of work. He never had time for a restaurant, and she didn't want to ask for fear of it sounding like a date. For his birthday, she'd brought two cartons of food and two sets of chopsticks from a Thai place near her apartment. He'd unwrapped the chopsticks and tried them for a minute before tossing them aside. His fuse was too short—his impatience too tried—to bother with the extra hassle.

She rubbed her feet against the carpet and hit the button to illuminate her iPhone. When Craig needed her, he'd send a text from his BlackBerry like he did during his meetings or between court appearances. When the latter happened, she liked to imagine him sitting in a row of lawyers in the courtroom, the waiting public slumped in the gallery behind him until they heard the words, "All rise."

But right now, her iPhone only showed her the wallpaper image of her cat. She glanced back through the darkened desks and saw his closed office door. By her calculation, three associates were still at work, but none of them worked for Craig. They sat in cubicles down partially illuminated hallways; people Koryn only saw when they walked past her to the elevator, keys jingling as they barely looked at her.

She tapped the Facebook icon on her phone and checked her messages there. A guy she'd met at a bar six months ago with her friend Tamara had sent her a smiley face. Koryn had been too polite to decline his Facebook friend request. Even as she'd chatted with him at the bar that night, she'd remembered a time when Craig had taken her in the backseat of his Lexus.

She scrolled to a new message from Tamara. *What color is your boyfriend's tie today?* Koryn smiled. She had told Tamara once, in a moment of weakness, that she wanted Craig to invite her to dinner—just some hint that she represented something other than casual sex. And he always had a different colored tie. She'd touched his ties several times, sliding them out of their knots and discarding them before she undressed the rest of him.

The phone vibrated beneath her fingertip, shivering in its sleek black case. She closed the Facebook app and saw a text from Craig. *Come in if you're not busy.*

She palmed the phone and slipped her feet back into her shoes, heading across the carpet to his office and opening the door.

Craig sat at his desk, his head in his hand as he looked at the glowing screen. He liked to keep the overhead light off, illuminating the room with only a lamp by his computer. He'd cleared his desk of papers and folders. He'd even tucked the framed photo of his daughter—the product of a distant divorce—into one of his drawers.

"Long day?" she asked.

He took a noticeable breath and swiveled his chair away from the computer. "Yeah. You?"

"I answer the phones. How long can my day be?"

He sat back in his chair, folding his hands in front of him as she felt the weight of his blue gaze on her. His face visibly softened when he looked her over like this. She saw it in the way his brow stopped furrowing and a small smile played on his lips. "Come here."

Her heels clacked on the floor as she walked around and leaned against the desk in front of him. He ran his hands up her legs, under the hem of her skirt, and rested them on her hips. His eyes looked large and different, softer somehow.

He reached her panties—red lace especially for this, for him—and slid them down her legs. Neither of them spoke. She stepped out of them, one foot at a time, before he lifted her and she sat on the edge of the desk.

No words were necessary as he pulled her forward so she fell back onto her elbows. She kept her eyes on him as he shoved her skirt to her hips, planting a stream of kisses along the inside of her thigh.

Already she breathed heavier. Already she bit the inside of her lip in anticipation. A dozen guys hitting on her at bars couldn't match this moment. She knew what his tongue would feel like when it reached between her legs and she held her breath when his mouth hovered over her.

"Come on," she hissed.

A light, slick flick of his tongue over her clit rewarded her, moving in little teasing circles.

She dropped her elbows out from under her and arched her back against the desk until her hair hung over the edge of the desk. He parted her legs and forced them into a V in the air. He always made her come like this. He insisted, even. Koryn secretly thought he loved the control—the ability to see how, in that moment, he'd won, even when he lost in court.

He slipped two fingers inside of her, moving them rhythmically as she felt that familiar feeling of him licking her to orgasm. A quiet, breathy moan felt heavy in her chest, but when it reached the air, it barely materialized. She wondered sometimes if she ever dripped on his desk, marking important documents with their secret. She'd certainly been wet enough, and undressed enough, and both were his fault.

Her thighs trembled when she came, and she gathered her breath to slide off the desk and drop to her knees. She always reciprocated for just as long, if not longer.

But there wasn't time. She felt his erection slip easily into her, pushing all the way to the hilt and causing another moan.

"I needed this," he whispered. "I needed to see you."

She opened her mouth to respond but he'd already established a rhythm, knocking his hips against her as she fondled her breasts through her dress. She kept her eyes closed, but she could feel his taking her in as she arched her hips and prayed for more.

It always felt deeper on the desk—smoother and more on target than anywhere else. She opened her eyes and the computer monitor blinked in her peripheral vision. She tilted her head and looked back at the blinds as she felt him dig his fingers into her hips and come deep inside of her.

They only waited a moment before she sat up. Even after work hours, they didn't stay like this for long. As she pulled on her underwear, she watched him adjust his tie. It was crimson today. Crimson like a rose petal.

She reached out and undid the knot, sliding off the tie and dropping it on the desk. "Work is over, you know."

He looked at the tie, his jaw firm, his hands drifting up and down her legs as if he needed the soft skin-on-skin contact. When he looked up at her, she tilted forward and kissed him. The softness sparked nerve endings, marking the dawn of new need.

He looked at her in close proximity. Koryn cleared her throat and willed herself to maintain eye contact. She wouldn't shy away from it. Not today.

"I want to go out for dinner this time," she said. "Not just sex. I want to date you."

His gaze slipped away from her and back again before he answered. For a long, tense moment, her heart beat heavy in her chest. *No,* she thought. *The answer is no.*

"Yeah," he said. "I've probably always wanted to ask you that."

Both of their smiles grew as she slid off the desk, waiting for him to grab his jacket before she took his hand and led him to the door.

"Down the street," she said. "I feel like Thai tonight."

OUCH!

Lily K. Cho

Ouch!" Josh roared. "Dammit, Susie, that hurt!"

He heard Susie giggle, but he didn't see her anywhere, so he turned back to the mirror and resumed his shaving.

Thwap.

"Susie! Stop that!" he yelled, rubbing his rear and twisting to inspect the two pink spots blooming on his ass. He looked around again, but still...no Susie. Only more giggling.

Thwap.

He jumped, stung, and heard Susie mocking him, "Does that sting, honey?"

So that's what this was all about, Josh thought with a grin. Payback for the spanking he had given her the night before. He smiled, remembering the way she had yelped with each smack of the paddle, the way her round little ass had turned cherry red. Another smile followed as he thought of how she had gone down on him after. But it hadn't been all about his enjoyment last night, not at all. He had spent the rest of the evening pleasuring her until she had come, gushing her white cream all over his face. Mmm...

Thwap.

The smack of the Nerf dart against the mirror startled Josh out of his reverie. His blue eyes narrowed briefly before he nonchalantly resumed his grooming. He knew Susie would show herself eventually; all he had to do was wait.

He heard a rustle and a creak and stole a glance in the mirror...aha!

He casually wiped the last of the shaving cream from his face and walked over to the bed. Suddenly he turned and whipped the closet door open. A squeal told him that he'd found her hiding place; a flash of light brown skin and Susie escaped. He looked down to find the Nerf dart gun on the floor.

"Oh, Susie," Josh called out, "did you forget something?"

"Oh, shit..." he heard from down the hall.

The hunter had become the hunted. Josh stalked his prey silently. He caught a glimpse of Susie's tan skin and fired a shot; another squeal, and then she was on the run again. He noticed she was only wearing a bra and panties.

Susie darted past him back into the bedroom, but Josh got his foot in the doorway before she could shut the door and lock him out. She was leaning hard against the door, putting all of her weight into it, and this made him laugh. Did she really think that she could stop him? Susie must have come to the same conclusion, because she suddenly darted from the door. Josh rushed into the room and tackled her before she could go anywhere. He tossed her onto the bed and straddled her, his thighs over hers. She tried to wriggle free, but he just casually leaned back, hands on hips, sitting on her.

He reached over to the nightstand drawer. Susie's brown eyes got wide and her pouty lips opened in an O. She started to struggle in earnest, twisting and bucking beneath him. "You wouldn't," she squeaked, "not the paddle again!"

But Josh had something else in mind, and it was the tethers that he'd gotten. He allowed her some freedom, and she did exactly what he had expected...turned over onto her hands and knees to try to crawl away. He shook his head and chuckled. She never learned...or maybe she just liked it that way; he hadn't really figured out which. He grabbed her arms and pulled them behind her, and she fell helpless onto the bed. He quickly removed her bra and bound her wrists, careful to keep his weight on her until he was done.

Josh grabbed her by the ankles and pulled her to the end of the bed. He slid her panties off and spread her legs, tethering her ankles to the bed frame so she couldn't move.

He went to the hall to retrieve the Nerf gun from where he had dropped it, leaving Susie with her bare ass up in the air. Perfect target.

Thwap.

"Ouch!"

Thwap.

"Stop it!"

Thwap.

"I am sooo going to kill you!"

Susie tried to struggle free, but Josh had her legs spread so wide she really couldn't do much.

Thwap.

Josh admired the way her smooth, round buttocks flinched with each impact. He loved her ass, the muscular lines, the soft spot where thigh and buttock met. He came up behind her and rubbed his hardening cock against her silky skin. Susie groaned and writhed, back arching to raise her ass higher.

Josh dropped to his knees behind her, his hands squeezing

her asscheeks. He heard her gasp and noticed that her skin was still a bit pink from the last night's paddling. "I'm sorry, baby," he said softly, placing kisses across her skin. The way her legs were spread exposed her smooth-shaven sex, and he ran his finger lightly up and down its outer folds; he loved the way her pussy lips would slowly open as she became more and more aroused. Suddenly he dove forward, attacking her captive cunt with his mouth, his tongue invading her, conquering her. She moaned and trembled as he thrust it deep.

"You want it, baby, don't you?" he asked harshly.

"Yes, yes, give it to me," was the breathless reply.

"You asked for it!" he said and gave her three quick, sharp smacks on the buttocks. Susie cried out in surprise and pain, tears coming to her eyes. The game had taken an unexpected turn. "Is that what you wanted?" Josh demanded.

"No!" Susie cried.

"Then what do you want? Tell me!"

"I want..." her voice trailed off. A light smack on her burning ass encouraged her to continue. "I want...you...to fuck me." Josh could hear the tremor in her voice, the embarrassment she always felt when he made her say it.

"Good girl," he whispered. He placed the tip of his hard cock against her open pussy and quickly shoved it in to the hilt. Susie moaned but did not complain. He rode her hard for a while, his cock plunging deep again and again. He could feel her getting wetter and wetter. His hands gripped her hips as he slammed into her.

"Oh god," she moaned, helpless to stop his almost brutal assault. But she liked it that way, and she urged him on. "Fuck me, fuck me!" she screamed, suddenly not so shy about it.

Josh reached around to finger her clit, and she screamed again as she came. Her orgasm hit her in waves, her muscles contracting around his cock. It was all he could do to keep from coming with her.

He untied her and knelt behind her again, kissing the red marks that covered her ass, then carefully licked at the petals of her swollen sex. He could feel her shiver. He gently fingered her sensitive clit, making her whimper. His tongue probed her pussy, lapping at her honey, bringing her down from the intense orgasm she had just experienced. She slowly rolled onto her back and smiled up at him. For a moment he wondered what she was up to, but one look into Susie's burning brown eyes and he knew that this was no longer a game.

Susie pulled him down for a kiss, slow and passionate and deep. Her legs wrapped around his waist, and he could feel her hot, wet pussy against his flesh. Slowly she began to grind against him, pulling him closer, until the tip of his shaft was at the mouth of her sex. Josh broke off from the kiss to gaze down at her, a finger gently stroking her cheek, then he slowly entered her. He watched as her eyes closed and her head angled back to expose her bare throat. Her lips parted slightly, and he heard her soft moan.

He held still inside her, savoring being in the woman he loved so much. She started grinding again, setting a slow rhythm. Her eyes opened and locked onto his. She began to smile that soft, loving smile of hers, but he started his own grinding motion, and the smile on her lips turned into a gasp of pleasure.

"Oh, Josh," she whispered, "my fierce, sweet love..." He could see the beginning of tears forming in her eyes, so intense was her emotion as she clutched at him.

Josh could tell that Susie was close again. He could feel it in the way her pussy tightened around him, tensing, squeezing... could hear it in her quickened breathing, how her moans were becoming more forced. Her hands gripped his shoulders and pulled him down onto her until he was almost crushing her. She held him close as her back arched. Her climax brought his own, and his shuddering spasms echoed hers until they both were left spent in each other's arms.

"Susie," he said tenderly, "I love you."

STEAM

Mariposa Cruz

J ust a few hours," Gwen assured Steve, who warily eyed the
garden reception at the Shadowridge Country Club, his
shoulders rigid with tension.

Steve had opted out of the Legacy Motors empire—as a
teacher, his summers remained open for renovation projects,
and his life was almost free of family entanglements. Even so,
he found facing the entire clan at once daunting, so he asked
Gwen to accompany him to the wedding.

"And you look amazing," she added, linking her arm with
his. Gwen resisted the urge to squeeze his muscled bicep. Steve
walked with the ease of a man comfortable in his own life. Who
knew her strictly T-shirt and jeans roommate could wear a char-
coal suit so well? The cobalt-blue shirt matched his eyes.

"Peach suits you; it makes your skin glow," he remarked
as the spring breeze lifted her skirt and exposed her long legs.
Despite the cool breeze, Gwen blushed under the intensity of his
gaze. *Don't ruin a perfect living situation with a midlife crush,*

she told herself. As a secretary who managed executive-size neuroses all day, it was relief to come home to a self-sufficient man with a wry sense of humor.

Shell-shocked by Nolan's abrupt departure and his engagement to a twenty-something, Gwen found a kindred spirit in an ad to share the rent and renovation of a three-bedroom bungalow downtown. In exchange for reduced rent, she spent her Saturdays pulling carpet, painting the walls or weeding the garden, slowly restoring the house and her life. The weekend renovations tanned and toned her body better than any gym or salon ever could.

Most of the women at the reception had long tresses or elaborate up-dos. Gwen nervously smoothed her dark bob.

"You hair looks fine," Steve assured her. "Do I have a hair out of place?" He tilted his shaved head toward her for inspection. Gwen laughed.

"It's your sister's wedding, try to be happy," she told Steve.

"Aside from the fact that Melissa abandoned her art to marry a corporate drone like our father, I'm ecstatic. She can create scrapbooks for her multitalented future offspring."

"I hope you're not using that line in your toast."

"I'll be good to the bride. As for everyone else, all bets are off." His thumb lightly caressed her palm.

"What do you mean?"

"You'll see." He winked at her. Before Gwen could press for details, the Hartley clan surrounded them. Steve's older brother, Marcus with his slick hair and slicker grin greeted her cordially while his wife Deirdre's lips curled in a semblance of a smile.

"So, how's the shack?" Marcus smirked.

"Still a work in progress," Steve replied.

"I can't believe how much the place has changed. He's so attentive to detail, it makes *such* a difference," Gwen exclaimed.

She squeezed his arm and beamed a knowing smile to Deidre. Marcus frowned at his wife who scowled in return.

"I'll grab us a couple of drinks," Steve murmured in her ear.

"I'd like that," she replied. Steve had just left her side, when she saw Nolan stroll toward her with his fiancée, Leigh. He traveled in the same circles Steve had fled, embracing the lifestyle her roommate loathed. With an excess of gel coating his diminished hair, he swaggered like a teenager with the prom queen on his arm. Gwen rubbed her arms against a chill, her insides in knots. With her life on track, why did she feel at loose ends around Nolan?

"Lovely wedding," Leigh trilled.

"We'll do something similar, but smaller, more intimate," Nolan said.

"Less costly," Gwen added.

Nolan frowned.

"Yes," Leigh agreed. A muscular arm encircled Gwen's waist. With Steve's strong body behind her, the knots inside her melted. Drawing her even closer, Steve introduced himself to Nolan and Leigh.

"I'm afraid this lovely lady owes me a dance. I'll have to steal her from you," he said. Steve guided her to an open spot on the dance floor. His touch was firm but light, his rhythm easy to follow, unlike Nolan who rigidly pulled her through every move then glared at her for not following his lead.

"I never figured you for a dancer," Gwen said. With a firm hand supporting her back, he spun her in a quick turn at the end of the song. She giggled at his wicked grin.

"Salsa is one of my many passions," he replied.

"What are your other passions?" The salsa faded into smooth jazz and Steve drew her closer.

"You," he whispered in her ear.

She shivered with exhilaration and terror. "When?"

"Since you appeared on my doorstep, but you seemed pretty fragile at the time." His hand caressed the length of her back. "Now that finally I have my hands on you, I don't think I can let you go." Warmth pooled in her belly as she leaned into him.

"I won't let you. What's next?"

"I have an idea. Follow me." Steve waved at a few family member members they passed as he led her to one of the far buildings.

"Tryst in a coat closet?" Gwen asked.

"Something better," he promised.

"You're kidding," she exclaimed, when they reached the men's locker room. Tossing his jacket and tie aside, he led her to one of the shower stalls and closed the curtain. Raising her chin slightly, he kissed her deeply. Heat swept through her while her fingers traced his muscled body. Aching for the feel of his bare skin, she fumbled with his clothes. Steve eased out of his shoes and pants.

"What if we get caught?" she gasped when he reached his briefs.

"It'll completely ruin my chance at membership, unless you'd rather wait." His fingers brushed her bare arm then stopped.

With her entire body on fire, waiting was not an option, so she slipped off the gauzy dress and removed her bra. Her nipples hardened in the sudden chill.

"Warm me up," she said.

His blue eyes gleamed as he gathered the rest of their clothes and shoes and tossed them outside the curtain. Gwen trembled as he stroked the curve of her breast, and then reached behind her to turn on the shower. He chuckled when she gasped at the shock of the cool water. The water soon warmed, pelting her back as he buried his face between her breasts. She moaned at the conflicting sensations, the rough brush of his goatee while his tongue circled her nipple then sucked on its rigid center.

"I want you now," she cried.

"Have to make sure you're warm."

He lathered her back, breasts and belly and then slipped his finger between her legs. Steam surrounded them as his finger traced the slippery folds, then stroked at the sensitive nub with increasing pressure. Shuddering, Gwen gripped his shoulders for support with one arm, while her other hand massaged his balls gently. Steve groaned while her fingers stroked the shaft of his cock.

"Hot enough?" she asked.

"God, yes."

He lifted her and she wrapped her legs around his broad back. Gwen gasped at his fullness as he entered her, then she kissed him deeply, her tongue exploring his mouth as he thrust inside her. She clenched her legs tight as the first wave of orgasm hit. He tenderly kissed her throat and shoulder as she collapsed against him. He gently lowered her back to the ground.

Silently they exchanged light kisses while they rinsed. "I can't wait until we're back at home," Steve said, as he wrapped her in a thick towel. He helped her with her dress and she straightened his tie.

"They'll know," Gwen said, as they walked toward the reception.

"Nonsense, you look radiant," Steve replied.

That's why they'll know.

His mother approached as they joined the other guests to wave to the happy couple. Her blue eyes narrowed with concern.

"Lovely wedding, you should be pleased," Steve remarked,

his arm tightening around Gwen's waist. His mother stared at them.

"You both are so flush—spending too much time outdoors without sunscreen," she said.

"You're right," he admitted.

"At your age, you can't be too careful." Steve nodded and she moved on to the other guests.

"Now that we're in the clear, only one question remains: your place or mine?" Gwen smiled at him.

"Both."

THE WAR
AT HOME

Giselle Renarde

Flipping onto her stomach, Brenda buries her face in the bunched-up pillow. *Too soft.* How can she possibly get to sleep with her head sinking into the oblivion of a dark-blue pillowcase? She can't breathe. Her mouth and nose are buried in feathers. She turns her head to the side, but that hurts her neck, so she flips again, landing with a bounce on her backside.

The sheets that match the pillowcase have wrapped themselves around her calves, and she kicks at them, but they don't let go. Growling, she kicks harder, but the sheets have her bound like a mermaid—just what Kaz always wanted. Thank god he's asleep.

Lucky bastard.

Sleep, just go to sleep! Brenda instructs herself. That hasn't worked all week; it probably won't work tonight. She should have exercised earlier, maybe some yoga after dinner or a sprint around the neighborhood. Anything to burn off this excess energy. But it's too late to run now. If she lies still, she's bound to drift off eventually.

She thinks about her sister, and the issue that started her sleepless nights—*the war at home*, as Kaz calls their spats. She can't believe how worked up she and her husband have become over an argument that rightly belongs to Brenda's sister. Once again, Rachel's insinuated herself into a dispute between the new beau and *his* ex-wife. Obviously Brenda has to take her sister's side, but Kaz doesn't think it's any of Rachel's business to get involved.

That's how this started, this bad blood between husband and wife.

It's just so *stupid*. No other word for it. Brenda tries to put her ire in a drawer, pack it away, but it just won't fit. And judging by the fact that Kaz is asleep right now and Brenda isn't, he's obviously succeeded where she's failed.

Stop thinking! It doesn't matter. Just go to sleep.

Her legs are still bound in the twisted blue sheet, and she kicks, kicks until she's sweating. Nothing happens. She's still trapped naked in these goddamn linens that are like seaweed drowning her mermaid self. And before she knows it, she's writhing in bed, flipping and twisting, screaming her frustration into the night.

Kaz bolts upright. "Whazzat?"

Brenda's heart stills so fast she wonders if she's having a heart attack.

Is he awake?

She thinks she might cry, though she doesn't know why. She tells him, "I'm stuck."

Kaz stares at her like he's wondering if she's a dream or if she's real. His ginger stubble glints gray in the moonlight, and she stares back. They stare at each other.

"My legs," she says when his gaze drifts across her naked breasts. "My legs are stuck in the sheets."

"Oh."

He's just looking at her now, at the curve of her belly, the tender slope of her breasts, her nipples pursed against the cool night air. He's watching the rise and fall of her body as it breathes. She watches him watching her.

But there's fire in her belly and she wants to revive this argument, though now is not the time. She wants to be right. She wants Kaz to *tell* her she's right. The words are important.

She bites her tongue.

Pushing the comforter to the foot of the bed, Kaz leans over and Brenda notices his erection firmly present beneath the sheet. There it is. Right there. Close enough to touch.

And she does.

Just as Kaz pulls down on the navy blue sheet, freeing her legs from its seaweed grip, Brenda grabs his cock and holds it. Just holds it, just grips the base and holds it. His tip seeps a clear pearl of precome. As it slides down that slit at the base of his cockhead, she dives in. She doesn't know why. In fact, she sees this happening from outside herself, from across the room, and all the while asks, *Why? Why am I licking him, sucking him, letting him win? Why?*

She hasn't consciously been holding out on him. It was more a matter of not wanting this, not wanting sex or touch or intimacy of any kind, not until he came around and admitted she was right.

Draping her breasts across his thigh, she curls her body around his and for the first time it occurs to her that maybe she *isn't* right. Her sister's always sticking that perfect little nose where it doesn't belong. It's not the most comforting notion— actually, it makes her feel like an idiot—but Kaz was right.

Fuck. He was *right*.

She laughs, and he asks, "What?" but she doesn't answer.

Instead, she tosses one arm around his shoulder and pulls herself up to his mouth, kissing him deeply. She won't let go of his cock, and he's still half-laughing while they kiss, but it's been almost a week since she's heard him laugh and she can't get enough.

His dick pulses in her grip, and her hand moves easily up and down the slick shaft. He probably wants her to bow into his lap and finish the job, but not tonight. Her pussy is a slick void, heavy with arousal, and she wants to feel him inside of her.

She wants it *now.*

Tossing one unstuck leg across Kaz's body, she straddles him, kneeling above his erection, teasing her clit with his cockhead.

"Oh god," she moans, as the heat of his smooth flesh plays against hers. She knows this doesn't do much for him, but it's heaven in high heels for her. Using his dick to stroke herself gives her that sense of feminine power she craves, and she gets herself damn near orgasm doing just this. Near, but not quite there. Something's missing, and she knows just where to find it.

Kaz grabs her hips, rocking them, pulling her down, down, down. "Fuck me, Bren."

"Fuck you?" she asks, and laughs. God, it feels good to laugh. "You want it bad, huh?"

"I want you so bad." He's tossing his head against the pillow like a bucking bronco. "So bad, Bren."

She can feel his need in her bones, and she gives herself to him, sinking slowly into his lap. When his mushroom head bursts into the wet warmth of her pussy, they both let out an urgent groan, like they couldn't keep it in if they tried. She descends on him, devouring more and more, until his fat tip bumps at the extreme depth of her.

Hissing, she eases up, away, but he grasps her ass and pulls her into the saddle of his hips. It doesn't hurt this time. A familiar warmth spreads through her belly and down her thighs as she takes him deep, riding his thick shaft slowly. She leans forward and presses the meat of her palm to Kaz's shoulder, heaves her body against his.

He says, "Play with your pussy," and she reaches down to find her clit fat and engorged. It throbs under her finger as she fondles it. She feels his slick cock entering her, pistoning up and down. He's driving it from below, bucking into her as she throws herself on him, crashing down. It's violent now, and that's how she wants it.

She scours her clit. Shouldn't take long. She's ready for this.

Her pussy clenches around his dick, milking that solid erection. He whimpers like a puppy. Her thighs feel the strain, but she keeps at it, rocking and tumbling, rubbing herself off. And then Kaz releases her hips and grabs her breasts with both hands. He flicks her nipples, then grasps them, then squeezes.

Something inside of her bursts, and the electricity is zapping all over, from her pelvis to her tits. Fuck, even her toes feel numb. She stops moving, except her hand—she's still working her clit hard, wanting to see how long she can draw out this orgasm. She wonders if Kaz came and she missed it. By the glazed look in his eyes, that's probably what happened.

Her clit twinges and cries *enough*, and she obeys, rolling off Kaz's body, letting his spent cock pop out of her pussy. Their thighs are damp with the juices of shared arousal, and Brenda concentrates on that sweet sensation of come dripping past her lips, down her asscrack, soaking the sheets.

"I didn't see that one coming," Kaz says. He's panting, out of breath.

Brenda's heart is still racing, but she smiles, peeling sweat-dampened strands of hair from her face. "Yeah, I know."

He takes a long inhale, and she's sure he's going to say something, but he doesn't. And she doesn't. But that's okay. She's not angry anymore.

She wraps one arm around him and settles her cheek against his chest. This is nice, much better than a too-soft pillow.

Yeah, this is perfect.

BY THE SEA

Angela R. Sargenti

I stop to get a new grip on the picnic basket, but she keeps walking toward the water ahead of me, her cute little ass swaying from side to side. She stops when she finds a spot she likes and starts bossing me around in a good-natured way. I set things up to her liking and she kicks off her sandals and wiggles out of her cutoff jeans.

"Well?" she asks, reclining on the blanket beside me. "Did you think about it?"

I look at her and smile.

Her eyes match the color of the sea and her hair's like golden floss, and it's hard to deny this woman anything.

I say, "A little."

"And?"

"And...I don't know."

"Come on," she tells me. "It'll be fun."

"I kind of have this thing about tight spaces."

She tosses her head back and laughs, then she looks at me

with a saucy grin and says, "I know. But I'll make it worth your while."

So I let her bury me in the sand.

"There," she says, tamping down the last bit and kissing me on the nose. "You're all set."

She sits down beside me in her cute little bikini, not saying a word, not doing a thing, and trapped there under all that sand, I know she's right about burying me.

It feels good to be helpless for a change, feels good to have no choice but to lie there under all that warm, solid weight.

To all outward appearances, she seems to be ignoring me, but I can tell she's really paying very close attention.

"I love you," she says quietly, never taking her eyes off the sea.

It's a brilliant day.

The water sparkles in the sun. A seagull cries out in triumph as he wheels about the sky, a French fry snatched from a small child in its claw. The pier is close enough to hear the clackety-clacking roller coaster climb, and the steady public scream of its descent.

We'll go there later, she and I, but for now I'm trapped.

Suddenly I remember an old monster movie I saw one time, filmed right here on this very beach. There was a monster spawned by radioactive sludge, and I know if it came to life now I'd be dead meat, for how could I fight it, or even run?

As if she knows what I'm thinking, she looks over at me and shoots me a naughty smile.

"Look at you," she tells me. "I could do anything I want to you."

Finally, she gets up.

She picks up the big beach towel we brought (that she made me carry, along with all the other gear) and wraps it around her waist. She tucks it together like a skirt and starts fumbling around under it, and I have no idea what she's up to until she drops her bikini bottom and kicks it aside.

She smiles at me as she moves closer. When she's right on top of me, towering over my head, she looks around, and then she sinks to her knees in the sand, covering my entire head with her towel.

It's still early in the year and this part of the beach is pretty deserted. I'm buried deep enough in the sand so it's hard to even tell I'm here, so I know we won't get busted for what I'm about to do to her.

I stick out my tongue and start exploring.

It's dark under the towel, but she wriggles around until she finds the right spot. Her folds are warm and pleasant and I smell her arousal, so I get to work at once, hands-free and eager to please. She tastes nice and fresh, and I like the way she grinds against my face.

I picture her smile and wonder what the other beachgoers see, what they think she's doing beneath her towel as she scootches around. My cock stirs to life, but packed in by all that sand, it's a pretty tight fit. I can still hear the roller coaster, but now the sound is muffled, out of range, a background noise at best.

My focus is on her now.

She moans. The sound travels down her body, straight through her pussy to my tongue, where it is felt more than heard, impossible to explain. She bucks forward a little faster now, though gently.

Almost too gently for my taste.

I wish my hands were free, because I would grab her and mash her soft little cunt against my face, smearing it this way and that, forward and backward and side to side.

She reads my mind again and makes some of those same

moves, rotating her hips in small round circles like she's doing a hula hoop or something. I hear another little moan of satisfaction and I know she's getting close, so close.

I shake my head no and nod yes, practically the only freedom of movement I'm allowed, and I think of another old horror movie, this time one where some deranged farmer tries to plant people up to their necks and grow them.

That farmer might think he's growing me, if he could get a look at my cock, which is so hard and trapped and dying to break free it's not even funny.

She stops a moment, and I hear someone's footfalls as they run by. She doesn't let that stop her for long, though, and she's back in action, her gyrations growing more insistent now. She wants to come, I know that, and I'm under her power as long as I'm buried, but I can prolong it.

I can draw back my tongue.

I can purse my lips.

I can stop rolling my head around beneath her, and I do.

She bobs up and down impatiently and clicks her heels against my head to urge me on, and I can't help smiling.

"Always in such a hurry," I whisper, and I know she hears me because she giggles and then she sighs. But it's a happy sigh, a sigh of contentment.

"I love the beach," she says aloud, and that's enough to spur me on. I stick out my tongue and she snaps to attention at once, rolling her hips and grinding her lovely cunt juice all over my face like she's riding a pony, or maybe one of those carousel horses from up there on the pier.

I love this so much I never want it to end. I want her to fuck my face forever, even though it's getting hot under here and I'm starting to sweat. No matter, though. Sweating is part of the point and I'd gladly burn in hell, if only I had her to ride me down.

Suddenly I feel her shudder, feel her cunt spasm. She reaches for a second one, though, and I oblige her by baring my bottom teeth and letting her scrape herself against them as hard or soft as she wants to.

She makes a small sound like she's out of breath, but she keeps going, scraping and scraping for a third until, finally sated, she shudders to a stop.

I hear someone else run by, and when the pounding footsteps die away, she stands up, her towel still wrapped around her waist. I close my eyes against the blinding sudden light and she falls to her knees beside me to shade me, using a corner of the towel to wipe my face.

The roller coaster roars down the track and people scream, but she just smiles.

"Want me to dig you out?" she asks.

And I say, "No. Not yet."

GARGOYLE LOVERS

Sacchi Green

'm siingin' in the raaiin..." But that song was from the wrong Gene Kelly movie, and it wasn't quite raining, and I was only whistling. My speaking voice gets me by, but singing blows the whole presentation.

Hal glanced down, her face stern in that exaggerated way that makes me tingle in just the right places. I shoved my hands into my pockets, skipped a step or two, and knew she felt as good as I did. Hal's hardly the type to dance through the Paris streets like Gene Kelly, especially across square cobblestones, but there was a certain lilt to her gait.

Or maybe a swagger. "That pretty-boy waiter was all over you," I said slyly. A gay guy making a pass always makes her day. "And giving me dirty looks every chance he got!"

"Lucky for you I'm not cruising for pretty boys, then. But don't give me too much lip or I might change my mind."

I couldn't quite manage penitence, but at least I knew better than to remind her that she already had a pretty boy, for better or worse. Still, some punishment games would be a fine end to the evening. Last night we'd been too jet-lagged to take proper advantage of the Parisian atmosphere. "That maitre'd with a beak like a gargoyle was sure eyeing me, too, especially from behind." I gave another little skip.

Hal ignored the bait. "Thought you'd had your fill of gargoyles today." A cathedral wouldn't have been her first choice for honeymoon sightseeing, but the mini-balcony of our rental apartment had a stupendous view of Notre Dame de Paris. I'd oohed and ahhed about gargoyles over our croissants and café au lait, so she'd humored me and we'd taken the tour.

To tell the truth, being humored by Hal unnerved me a bit. I didn't want being married to make a difference in our relationship. The fact that she'd shooed me out of that sex toy shop in Montmartre while she made a purchase was reassuring, but just in case, I decided I could manage some genuine penitence after all.

I hung my head and peered up at her slantwise. "I know I was a real pain. I can't figure out what it is about gargoyles that just gets to me. They're sort of scary, but not really, and sort of sad, and some of them are beautiful in a weird kind of way." Just as Hal was, but I'd never say that. "I'm sorry I went on about them like that."

"What makes you think they're sad? Just because their butts are trapped in stone?" She was trying to suppress a grin. I felt better.

"Well, I'd sure hate that, myself!"

That got me the squeeze on my ass I'd been angling for. "I'd rather have these sweet cheeks accessible," she said. The squeeze got harder than I'd bargained for, startling me into a grimace.

She eased off with a slow stroke between my thighs. "You should have seen your face just now. Could be there's something like that going on with the gargoyles. Not rage, or fear, or pain at all—unless it's pain so delicious it makes them howl with lust."

I was awestruck. Hal is generally the blunt, taciturn type, but I love it when her wicked imagination bursts forth. Almost as much as I love the vulnerability that once in a while gives an extra gruffness to her voice.

She was on a roll now, face alight like that of a gleeful demon. A lovable demon. "There's somebody hidden behind the stone, in another dimension, or time, or whatever, giving the gargoyle the fucking of its life. A reaming so fine it's been going on for centuries."

"Yes!" I was very nearly speechless. To lean out high above Paris, in the sun, wind and rain of eons, my face forever twisted in a paroxysm of fierce joy while Hal's thrusts filled me eternally with surging pleasure...

A few drops of rain began to fall, but that wasn't what made us hurry faster across the Pont Saint-Louis. The great ornate iron gates at our apartment building had given me fantasies that morning of being chained, spread-eagled, against them, but now I rushed across the cobblestoned courtyard and through the carved oak door, so turned on that the four flights of stairs inside scarcely slowed me down—which might also have been because Hal's big hand on my butt was hurrying me along.

At our apartment, though, she held me back while she opened the door. "Over-the-threshold time. It'll be more official when we get back home, but this will have to do for now."

So I entered the room slung over Hal's shoulder, kicking a little for balance, until she dumped me amongst the red and gold brocade cushions on the couch. They went tumbling off as I struggled to get my pants lowered.

"Not here," she mused. "Maybe up there?" There was a sturdy railing across the loft that held the king-size bed.

"Out there! Please?" The balcony was really only a space

where the French windows were set back into the wall about a foot, but there was an intricate iron fence along the edge, and with the windows wide open it had felt like balcony enough at breakfast time.

"Can you be quiet as a gargoyle?"

"You can gag me."

"No. I want to see your face." Hal pulled open the windows, grabbed the bag from the sex toy store, heaved me up, and the next minute I was kneeling on the balcony and clutching the fence.

She moved aside a couple of pots of geraniums and tested the fence for strength and anchoring. "This would take even my weight," she muttered. In seconds she'd fastened my wrists to the railing with brand-new bonds that looked uncannily like chains of heavy iron links, even though weren't hard as metal and had just a hint of stretch to them. "Feel enough like a gargoyle?"

"Mm-hm." I was drifting into a space I'd never known before. Lights from the Quai d'Anjou below and the *quais* across the Seine were reflected on the dark river, flickering like ancient torches as the water rippled past. Even the lights of modern Paris on the far bank took on a mellow glow that could have fit into any century.

"Hold that thought." Hal backed away into the room. I scarcely heard the rustling of the shop bag or the running of water in the bathroom. Then she was back, soundlessly, a dark looming presence that might have been made of stone.

The night air drew me into its realm. I leaned out over the railing as far as my bonds would allow, my butt raised high. Then Hal had one arm around my waist, holding me steady, while her other hand probed into my inner spaces that she knew so well. Need swelled inside me and shuddered through my body, catching in my throat as strangled, guttural groans. My face twisted with the struggle not to make too much noise, my mouth gaped open and my head flailed back and forth.

A whimper escaped when her hand withdrew, and so did a short, sharp bleat as something new replaced it: smooth, lubed, not quite familiar, not any of Hal's gear I'd felt before. I heard her heavy breathing, felt her thrusts and lost all sense of anything beyond the moment, anything beyond our bodies. A scream started forcing its way up through my chest and throat.

Just in time, Hal snapped open the bonds on my wrists, lifted me from behind, and lurched with me across the plump back of the couch. With a rhythm accelerating like a *Parisienne's* motorbike she finished me off, then found her own slower, deep pace, and her own release. I could still barely breathe, but I managed to twist my neck enough to see her contorted face at that moment. Yes, magnificently beautiful in its own feral way.

In the aftermath we curled together, laughing when she showed me the new gargoyle-faced dildo. "Those French don't miss a trick when it comes to tourists," I said.

Hal grew quiet. I thought she was dozing, but after a while she cleared her throat. "Those French..." Her voice was unusually gruff. She tried again. "They claim to be tops in the lover department, too, I've heard. But I've got the best deal in the whole world with you. The best lover..." She stroked my still-simmering pussy. "The prettiest boy..." She touched my cheek. "The best wife...and the wildest gargoyle in all of France."

I remembered her face just minutes before and knew that the last part wasn't true. Still, the wisest response seemed to be a kiss that moved eventually from her mouth along her throat, and lower, and lower, with more daring than I'd ever risked before, and eventual proof that the best lover part, at least, was absolutely certain.

BEST FRIENDS

Catherine Paulssen

Jake looked up from his laptop when his phone rang. "Tatum!"
"Are you still at that coffee place?" his friend's voice came
tinny through the speaker.

"I am."

"I'm not sure if I can make it in time."

"Where are you?" he asked. "This line is terrible!"

There was a pause. "I'm still out...with my bike."

"At Hot Springs?"

"Uh-huh."

"The movie starts in an hour," he said, checking his watch.
She exhaled.

"Tatum, what is it?" The line crackled. "Tate?"

"I had an accident," she said, her voice raised.

"Are you all right?"

"Yes, I'm okay. But my bike chain is broken."

He turned toward the tilted window. The air hung heavy

between the blocks of houses. Across the street, a vendor was packing away his display. "It will be pouring soon! Where are you?" He waited for her answer, and when it didn't come, waved at the waiter. "Tate, stop being stubborn. Where are you?"

"I'm off Stonebridge Road. Western tip of Desoto Lake."

"I'll be right there."

The winds had already flared up when he got into his car, and the streets emptied as he drove out of town. The sky behind him was still bluish gray, and lit with a pale shine, but above the green slopes of Hope Springs, the leaden mass seemed to touch the tips of the trees.

A flash of golden light streaked over the lush landscape, followed by distant rumbling. Another bolt of lightning painted the sky pink, then raindrops started splattering on his windshield. Within seconds, the streets were covered with a shimmering film. He cursed, thinking of Tatum amid this violent storm, and that he would need to slow down if he wanted to make it to her safely.

Finally, the lights of his car fell on her slim figure in the drenching rain. She had her arms wrapped around her body, her shorts clung to her legs, and her copper-colored hair hung in long, wet streaks over her shoulders, but she made no move to get into the car. He leaned over and pushed open the door of the passenger's side. "Come on!" he called out to her, and she came to the door.

"What about my bike?"

"No one will steal your bike in this weather! We'll fetch it tomorrow."

She frowned, then turned and sprinted back to the bike.

"Tatum! Get away from the trees!"

"Well, help me!" she yelled back.

For a moment, he watched her attempts at hiding the bike behind a tree trunk, her shoulders hunched. He rolled his eyes and got out of the car, wrapped his arms around her from behind and carried her away, ignoring her protests. He pushed her into the car and slammed the door shut. Soaked to his bones, he fell in the driver's seat and threw her a glace, both annoyed and amused. She opened her mouth, but shut it again. A flash, like sizzling veins, streaked out over the sky.

"I needed to practice for the tour," she said eventually, her lips puckered.

"Can't do it if you die of pneumonia first."

She grimaced. "Don't be worse than my mom!"

"There's a fresh shirt in my sports bag," he grinned. "On the backseat."

She crawled to the back and Jake's eyes flickered to the rearview mirror. He'd found her attractive for a long time. But friends didn't peek at each other while changing. He turned his eyes back on the road.

"Let's watch the thunderstorm move on over the park," she said, her words muffled as she pulled his shirt over her head.

He took a deep breath and turned the car to the top of a small hill. Tatum patted the bench. "Come." She kept her eyes fixed on the spectacle outside while he crawled on the seat next to her. "Look at that... I wish there were more thunderstorms," she mumbled, her breath fogging the window.

Jake got out of his drenched shirt as another flash lit the inside of the car. She snuggled against him and reached for his hands to wrap them around her. For some moments, he just held her, and the warmth of her rolled through him. He could smell the traces of rain on her skin and feel his breath mingling with the scent of her body.

"Why are you so bullheaded?" he asked, resting his chin on

her shoulder.

"Because..." She shifted a little and played with his fingers. "Because I don't want people to think I can't handle things on my own."

"People? It's just you and me."

She gnawed on her bottom lip for a moment and waited for the thunder to die down. When she turned her head, a curious glance lay in her eyes. "It's just you and me."

Her breath brushed his lips. He thought he saw a flush of pink on her cheeks. Very carefully, he tugged a strand of her hair out of her face. A drop of water ran down his hand.

Tatum sneezed. She gave him an apologetic smile. "We're still in our wet duds." She got out of her shorts, shoes and socks, and when they were almost naked, snuggled her head against his chest and wrapped herself around him. "Thank you," she murmured.

"Hm?"

"Thank you for picking me up."

He pressed a kiss on her hair. "Always." Her hair tickled his chest and he wondered if she could hear the pounding of his heart over the thick drops thrumming on the car's roof. Blood rushed to his crotch and into his fingertips. "Tate..."

Instead of answering, she cuddled herself even closer into his embrace. She sighed faintly when his cock, bobbing against his briefs, nudged her thigh. She kissed his neck. A second kiss followed, and a third, and now her teeth nibbled at his earlobe. She made a trail of kisses up his throat, kissed his temple, the spot behind his ear. Her mouth grazed his cheek, but before she had reached his lips, Tatum stopped and searched his eyes. She cupped his face then pressed a soft kiss on his lips. He grabbed her butt and pulled her close, deepening the kiss.

His fingers ran over her back. When their lips parted, she

stripped off the shirt and leaned back a little in his arms, allowing him to let his eyes wander over her bra, so damp he could see through the pale-pink fabric, see the outline of her hardened, dark nipples. He moved one cup aside and grazed the goose bumps of her skin with his nose and lips. Tatum moaned as he enclosed the nipple with his lips, and buried her fingers in his hair.

Her skin was softened and chilly where the soaked clothes had been, and his fingers wandered over it as if touching a woman's curves for the first time. "You feel wonderful," he whispered against her breast.

Tatum sighed into his hair then broke away from him with gentle force. She placed another kiss on his mouth and let her fingers crawl underneath his briefs to massage his balls. Giggling while trying to maneuver in the small space of his backseat, she slipped out of her thong and stripped him of his briefs. She gave his cock a little kiss and threw Jake a mischievous glance from underneath her lashes. Then she got up again and lowered herself on his lap. She moved in slow circles, commanding a rhythm that drove him to the edge again and again yet never sent him over it. He tamed his own agitation and let her take of his thrusts what she needed until he felt her close to erupting.

Her breath became ragged, her moans wilder; she abandoned the controlled rhythm and finally collapsed into his embrace, a contented sigh on her lips.

They stayed in each other's arms until the rain subsided. Not a word was spoken, not when they got dressed, not when they climbed back into the front of the car. The countryside's green shone with new depth, cleansed from the heat of the day. Drops of rain glistened in the treetops and the bushes around them.

"Drive me home?" she asked.

He nodded. "Sure."

"Will you spend the night?"

He gave her a long look. There was a shyness in her eyes he hadn't seen before. He nodded and leaned in to kiss her. With a smile, she snuggled into her seat as Jake started the car and drove toward the town, which lay silently in the valley.

DIRTY LAUNDRY

Martha Davis

Joshua Moran is an intimidating six-foot-four, two-hundred-and-fifty-pound, power-tool-loving, Dodge-pickup-driving, rare-steak-eating fireman who grunts loudly as his favorite method of showing displeasure. When we first moved in together, my best friend said, "I believe you when you say he's absolutely amazing in bed. Just look at the sheer gusto he puts into everything else he does. But there is no way that Neanderthal can be domesticated."

She won the century's most-shocked award when I proved her wrong. All it took was a little ingenuity, and in no time, I found a way to get Josh to do his share of the household chores. Yesterday, he did the laundry.

I wore a seen-better-days, tattered gray bathrobe when I wandered into his domain—the living room. I stood in front of the big-screen TV with my hands planted firmly on my hips and my breasts purposely thrust in the air.

"Honey, can you carry the laundry basket down into the

basement? It's too heavy for me."

Josh grunted, the tone and swiftness letting me know he was pleased. Neanderthal man enjoys every opportunity to prove his physical superiority over tiny cave girl, and he eagerly lugged it down the small flight of wooden steps, dropping it by the washing machine.

"Sweetie, I was thinking. It's been a long day and I'm kind of tired. Why don't you do the laundry and I'll supervise?"

He grunted. This time longer in length and from deeper in the throat. Less pleasure.

"Here," I added, stripping off the bathrobe and throwing it in the basket. "You'll need to wash this, too. Just toss the whites in the corner for now and load the colors."

Seeing me dressed in nothing but a see-through open-mesh, red chemise with matching G-string made him a lot more agreeable to my request. As he worked, I ran my fingers slowly over his broad back, my hands moving up and down the warm flesh over hard muscle. I planted kisses haphazardly up the length of his spine, fully aware I was starting the spark for a potential five-alarm fire.

I pressed my breasts into his back, reached under his arms and around his chest to tickle his nipples. My fingers worked a path down to the hard, unyielding muscle of his lower belly and played with the tuft of soft hair splattered there like silk down on sculpted stone.

I stood on tiptoes and whispered, "Looks like your clothes are dirty, too. You'll have to take them off and toss them in." Then I nibbled on his earlobe and giggled all girly-like.

Josh made record time stripping naked and dumped the clothes, still warm from the heat of his body, and what little remained of the clothing in the basket into the washing machine. A couple of white pieces made it into the mix but when a girl has a giant naked Adonis in eyesight, she has little concern for pink socks.

As he measured the soap and started the cycle, I toyed with his naval and moved my hand down to play with his hardening dick. It was so smooth and silky to the touch. I wrapped my palm around it, feeling it harden even more. He let me stroke and pet it until it became so hard the veins were pronounced and a drop of come rose from the little dent in the dark head.

I caught the first of his passion on the tip of my index finger and brought it to my lips, "Mmm."

"That's enough!" Josh growled.

He swooped me up and tossed my G-string-covered ass on the washing machine. He pressed his body into mine and I was trapped between the hot hardness of his body against my belly and between my legs, and the cold steel of the machine against my backside. My body melted into his and he kissed me, his palms stroking the bare skin of my upper arms.

"I want you to lick my pussy," I said into his mouth. He braced my hips and shoulders and slid me back into a better position.

Covering my lips and cheeks with wet kisses, he trailed a path down my cheek and jaw, to my supersensitive throat, where he nuzzled me with his lips and teeth. He sucked hard, purposely bringing up a hickey to mark me as his. It wasn't the first time, and I loved the feel of his mouth at my throat too much to ever demand it be the last.

His hands slid under my chemise and his callus-roughened palms cupped my breasts. He taunted my left nipple with his thumb and index finger until I moaned and wiggled closer against his groin.

Josh's teeth found my right nipple through the chemise fabric and increased the blaze already completely beyond control. Me, worry? Nah! My Neanderthal fireman is an expert in heating me up and putting out the flames. Over and over again. He lowered his upper body and I felt the moist warmth of his breath through my panties. I ached to feel his mouth and fingers there.

He slid my sodden panties to the floor and used his fingers to open me wide. The cool air on my heated and exposed naughty bits inspired widespread goose bumps. His lips massaged my labia and his tongue slid between my slippery folds. He brought the tip of his wet tongue close enough to tickle my swollen clit, but pulled back before actually touching it, teasing me like I had done him moments earlier. Only worse.

I writhed beneath his tongue, his firm grip on my thighs. My moans and sighs begged for more. I gasped hard when he finally gave in to my demands and made contact with my clit.

"Yes, Josh. Please," I cried out, wiggling closer to his mouth.

He played expertly with my pussy, probing me with two fingers as his tongue fluttered rapidly on my clit and the washing machine began to bounce and grind under my butt.

I flung my arms back over my head, slamming my palms against the cement wall behind the machine. "Fuck me, Josh. Damn it, fuck me!"

I was on fire. I couldn't take any more and desperately needed rescue. He knew. He stood up straight and pressed his thick cock against my pussy, tapped at my clit a few more times with the head and slid the whole thing slowly into my wetness. I grinded against him as he worked it in and out, the whole time begging to be taken deeper and harder, as loud and breathless as he needed to get him off, too.

My hero gave me exactly what I wanted and then some, hard and fierce. I convulsed in orgasm, the spasms of my body milking his cock still stuffed to the hilt inside me. He pulled out, stroked his dick, and made it spew come all over my lower belly, pussy, and the hem of my chemise, again marking me as his. I rubbed it into my skin in slow circles like lotion while he watched.

I've heard rumors around the firehouse, gossip from the wives and girlfriends, that all the effort I put in to getting Josh to do chores really isn't necessary. All those big, burly firemen have to keep the firehouse spic and span and keep dinner on the table for the whole crew and he's as much a domestic god as he is a god in bed. But I don't mind. And I know he's onto my game and doesn't mind, either.

Today, I'm giving that Neanderthal a blow job—I mean, cooking lessons—out on the grill. As if he needs any help controlling an open flame.

NIGHT MOVES

Christine d'Abo

N o, no, no, *no, no!*"

I couldn't tell you what the nightmare had been about specifically. Images of too-tall walls and frantic running through black hallways were all that lingered as I blinked madly into the dark of our bedroom. The soft whooshing of the ceiling fan and the gentle rubbing of my husband's hand against my back did little to slow my pounding heart. My stupid brain wouldn't shut off.

"You 'kay, babe?"

"Yeah." I reached for the hair elastic on my nightstand that I'd yanked from my hair before bedtime. I hastily threw my hair into a ponytail. "Just hot."

"Mmm."

The sheets had twisted around my legs and waist, cocooning me in place and sending my temperature soaring. It took longer than it should to kick myself free.

"Fucking thing." I flopped back against the bed and let my eyes fall shut.

The moment sleep threatened to overtake me again, my heart began to pound once more and the images drifted back. Running, faster, faster, can't get away. *No!*

"Baby, wake up."

I'm not sure I was even able to open my eyes at first. One moment I was running down a hallway and the next I found myself pressed hard against my husband's chest.

His fingers made their way into my hair, as he scratched my scalp and made cooing noises. The terrified shudders eventually gave way to tingles of pleasure. I pressed my nose into his skin and pulled in a deep breath. His chest hair tickled my face even as his familiar scent steadied my nerves.

"You okay now?" He pressed a kiss to my temple.

I've never been one for bad dreams, not since early on in our relationship. I'd grown more confident in not only myself, but in us as a couple. Every challenge we'd faced, we'd pulled through and had come out the other side stronger than before. But recently with the threat of me losing my job and the daily stress of having two teenage girls in the house, I found that confidence slowly eroding.

"I don't know." And didn't that hurt to say, a whispered confession in the dark.

"This about work?"

"Maybe." I snuggled in as he tightened his hold on me. "Too tired to talk."

"Hmm."

The ceiling fan had begun to lull me back to sleep when he shifted in my arms. The press of his cock against my stomach wasn't much of a surprise. I was practically naked. To hell with the time, that was pretty much the unwritten invitation to his body to wake up and take notice. *Hello, horny man!*

He shifted back trying to put some distance between us. I

could almost hear him justifying the move. *It's the middle of the night. She has to be up early for work. The dog might wake up and freak out. She won't be into it.*

I'm not sure if it was my need to finally chase the nightmare away, or simply the appeal of sleepy sex that had me reaching for his cock. God, I loved that he slept naked.

"Sorry." He kissed the top of my head. "You don't have to."

"Maybe I want to."

"Hon, you have work—"

I tugged on his shaft, which shut him up instantly. My fingers were sticky from dried sweat, making it difficult for me to stroke him. I wasn't in the mood for a blow job, but a little oral lubrication would go a long way to making this pleasant for both of us. Pushing the sheet down the rest of the way, I shifted so I could suck his head into my mouth. The fingers still in my hair clenched as I bobbed slowly up and down his cock.

The taste of sweat and precome filled my mouth, making it water. There was no pressure to go fast, no worries of being interrupted. I took my time, savoring the sensations and enjoying his quiet groans and gasps.

He tugged lightly on my hair. "C'mere."

I let his shaft go with a soft *pop* and climbed on top of him. As much as I normally loved the feeling of his body pressing mine into the mattress, tonight I needed to be the one in control. I pulled off my T-shirt, thankful for my lack of panties. Guiding his tip to my pussy, I sunk down onto his shaft in an easy move. The feeling of being filled comforted me in a way that had nothing to do with the act and everything to do with the man below me. This was real. This connection, the two of us making love in the dark.

With his hands on my hips, he let me set the pace. I hadn't

been aroused until I felt him squeeze me and mutter encouragement, then my body ignited. I needed to come, wanted to share the pleasure with him in this stolen moment.

"Grind down on me. Yeah, like that. You're so fucking hot."

He slid one hand from my hip to my breast, pinching and teasing my nipple. With each tweak it felt like a shot straight to my clit. The pressure built, but my sleepy body didn't want to cooperate. Frustration was my old enemy, one I couldn't easily do battle with tired.

"Can't." I squeezed my eyes shut.

"Relax." He shifted his other hand between my legs to press his thumb to my clit. "There's no rush. That's it."

My body did as he said, and the lingering blackness of my dreams finally dissipated. Keeping me in place, he sat up and latched on to my breast, his tongue picking up where his fingers left off. He kept the pace steady but slow, stoking my pleasure higher with every gentle swipe. He knew me and my body so well that even in the grip of sleep he could coax a response from me like a beloved instrument.

It was my turn to cling to him, digging my nails into his back as my orgasm burst from me. Pleasure rolled through my body, each wave growing stronger, until it finally stopped with a shudder.

Releasing my breast, he grabbed my hips once more and pounded up into me. I reached behind him to grab the headboard, needing the leverage to keep my body where he wanted it. My mouth was aligned with his ear, and I leaned in to suck on his lobe. I loved the sounds he made when I did that.

"Fuck," he muttered and dropped his forehead to my shoulder. Heat from his body made mine slick with sweat. Not that I cared.

He latched on to my shoulder and groaned into my skin as he pumped his release into me. I held on as long as I could until I knew he was done and we could both fall back onto the mattress. We were sticky with sweat and come, our bodies glued together and to the sheets. It was wonderful.

"Want me to get you a washcloth?" He pushed my hair from my face and kissed my mouth, my cheek. "Might help cool you down."

"No, that's fine."

He got up anyway.

The press of the cool cloth against my face and neck, the insides of my thighs and between my legs, soothed me. Like so many times before, when I needed him to, he was there taking care of me. When he crawled back in bed, I was maneuvered onto my side so he could spoon against my back.

"Better?" His whispered words already betrayed his sleepiness.

"Yup."

"No more bad dreams. We'll figure this out too."

"I know." I did know, but having his body wrapped around mine gave me the reassurance I'd needed. "I love you."

"I love you too, sweetie. Now go to sleep so you're not bitchy in the morning."

I lay awake in his arms for several more minutes until his soft snores vibrated against my neck. It would be okay. We would get through this the same way we got through everything in our lives. Letting out a soft huff, I tugged his arm a little closer against my chest, closed my eyes and went to sleep.

MISS
ORGANIZED

Elizabeth Coldwell

The calendar alarm sounded as Gail sought the best way to word a polite email to a rude client. Startled by the loud, persistent ringing, she stared at the notification that had popped up on her screen. *Seven P.M.—spanking.*

Her first thought was, how had it gotten to be seven without her realizing it? She really needed to make a start on dinner, unless Matt had taken over the chore as he did so often these days. Thoughtful, practical, willing to take a backseat to her career—she really was lucky to have him in her life.

Reading it a second time, the real implications of the note hit her. *A spanking?* She might be meticulous about recording every appointment, every deadline in her calendar, but she couldn't remember scheduling anything like this. Just as she was wondering whether she ought to run her antivirus software and change her passwords in case she'd somehow been hacked, there was a sharp rap at the door.

"Come in," she called, distracted by the mysterious notification. The door opened and Matt stepped inside, but it was a version of her husband she barely recognized. He wore a tweed jacket she'd never seen before, a white shirt and a loosely knotted tie, and his normally rumpled blond hair was slicked back with gel. The effect of the outfit was to give him an air of off-kilter authority, like a teacher with his own, unorthodox ways of keeping an unruly pupil in line.

"I'm here for our appointment," he announced.

Gail glanced at her calendar. "You—you scheduled a spanking for me?"

She didn't know whether to be annoyed or amused at this flagrant misuse of her time. Though it *was* seven o'clock on a Friday night, she had to remind herself. She should have been off the clock well before now. And the thought of Matt putting her over his knee so he could smack her bottom was sending a flood of sticky heat into her panties and making her shift anxiously in her seat.

"Your behavior's a cause of concern." Matt walked over to the desk, picking up a wooden ruler and toying with it in a manner that made Gail wonder whether he might be contemplating using that on her backside. "You have no time for anything but your work, you leave me to do the chores... Frankly, it's not good enough. You might pride yourself on being Miss Organized, but you need to be taught what your real priorities should be."

His points hit home—they really hadn't been spending enough time together over the last couple of months, in bed or out of it—and a guilty flush heated her cheeks. Before she could raise her voice to respond, he caught her arm, pulling her to her feet so he could take her place on her sturdy office chair. Half-giggling, half-afraid—though she'd admitted on many occasions how much the thought of being spanked by Matt turned her on, it had remained an intriguing fantasy till now—she allowed him to pull her onto his lap, bottom up.

Even Matt's cologne was different tonight, she realized as she breathed it in, lying still in the moment before he inched her skirt up the backs of her legs. Something old-fashioned, making her think of sun-warmed wood and the sea. He'd taken the time to create a whole new persona for this encounter, and she couldn't help but admire his ingenuity. Then she felt his fingers hook into the waistband of her panties, bringing her back to awareness of her precarious position.

"Hey," she objected, "you never said anything about spanking my bare bottom!"

"You know it's for your own good," he replied, the words sending another little thrill of excitement through her. It didn't stop her wriggling and kicking her legs, trying to make the task of pulling her underwear partway down her thighs as difficult as she could.

Once he'd succeeded in baring her to his satisfaction, Matt smoothed his palm over her exposed cheeks, lulling her with the gentle, repetitive caress.

"So, Miss Organized, I'm going to give you an even dozen smacks. Do you think you can count them for me?"

It sounded like such a simple thing to do. "Yes, Sir."

When the first swat landed, the flat of his hand smacking audibly against her buttock but not really hurting, she wondered why she'd been worried. "One."

The second, third and fourth were just as manageable, sending a pleasant warmth through her flesh and making her writhe just a little on Matt's thick thighs. Beneath her she felt the solid, swollen bar of his cock, and knew the sights and sounds of her punishment were getting to him, just as she'd expected they would. What she hadn't expected was that he'd raise the force and tempo of his slaps, swinging his arm harder so every blow cracked sharply against her ass. She counted the strokes through gritted teeth, trying not to yell out loud and wondering if her skin looked as hot and red as it felt.

Matt said nothing, just kept on spanking her, reserving the last two swats for the place where her asscheeks met the tops of her thighs. Now her resolve did break, and she squealed and sobbed as pain melded with pure, sweet pleasure.

"That hurt," she complained, fighting the urge to reach behind her and rub her sore ass.

"It was supposed to. But you needed it, didn't you?"

"Yes, Sir." Strange as it sounded, she had. She'd needed something to take her away from the pressures of work and the imperative to do anything other than submit to Matt's deepest desires—and her own. Now that it was over, all she wanted was for him to satisfy the ache between her legs, an ache more insistent than that in her punished cheeks.

In tune with her needs and driven by his own, Matt helped her to her feet and encouraged her to bend over the desk. Her neat, organized piles of paperwork, folders and to-do tray seemed to mock her as she waited, but she ignored them. Work no longer mattered; this was playtime.

From behind her came the grating rasp of a zip, then rustling as her husband's jeans came down. Without ceremony, he spread her legs wider, lining up his cock at the entrance to her wet, waiting pussy. With a smooth stroke, he entered her, pushing all the way inside until their bodies were so intimately joined she didn't know quite where she ended and he began. She always loved this moment, when he held her close before beginning to fuck, hard and steady. Every stroke pushed her against the edge of the desk, but she needed the ferocity, the ruthlessness with which Matt took her. Reaching beneath her, she put a finger to her clit and rubbed, hard and fast, in time with his thrusts. Lost in bliss, she felt herself convulse around

Matt's thick length, his orgasm following moments behind her own.

He nuzzled her neck, hugging her close. "I love you so much, Miss Organized."

"And I love you...Sir."

"So," he asked, apparently keen to clear up one last thing before he broke role and went to finish the dinner, "do you think you've learned your lesson not to work so hard in the future, and not to neglect your husband?"

"I think so, but you may need to give me a reminder from time to time."

His chuckle told her that was just the answer he'd been hoping to hear.

WHEN THE VACATION IS OVER

Annabeth Leong

It started when Amy took Paul's hand while standing in front of the enormous Buddha statue on Hong Kong's Lantau Island. If she had been home, she would never have done something like that. She would have focused on their differences—his dark skin compared with her light, his glasses versus her contacts, and his having traveled there as a sort of pilgrimage rather than, like her, visiting the statue simply because the guidebooks recommended it.

Now, in a foreign country, Amy's definition of common ground had transformed completely. She sat next to Paul on the crowded, careening bus to the Po Lin Monastery because he looked American, and smiled in genuine delight when she discovered they were from "the same place"—though normally she would have said South Florida and Central Florida might as well have been two different countries.

Standing on the steps leading up to the bronze statue's smiling abundance, taking pictures of each other, then angling their cell phones awkwardly to take pictures of themselves together, Amy glanced at Paul and saw in his face the same joy, freedom and wonder she felt in her heart. She reached for him naturally, before she thought about it.

The rest of the day, they walked hand in hand, without saying anything about the change between them. On the return bus ride, she napped on his shoulder.

It wasn't until later, alone in her tiny bed at the Emperor, that she allowed herself to reflect on the delicious warmth of him beside her and the way it had made her shiver every time he squeezed her hand.

He called her in the morning. He wanted to see the Ten Thousand Buddhas Monastery. Soon, Amy found herself beside Paul on a never-ending staircase, climbing up the side of a mountain through greenery so lush and vivid that she was sure she would not be able to remember its true beauty. Gold statues of the Buddha posted on every step seemed as unique as snowflakes and Paul made guesses at their spiritual meaning while Amy tried to understand how such similar objects could be shaped by human hands to look so distinct.

At the top of the stairs, in the square before the temple proper, she took Paul's hand again and used it to pull him closer. In a land of foreign fragrance, he smelled of familiar soap. She pressed her nose to the soft fabric of his shirt, breathing against his muscled chest, her heart suddenly pounding. After a moment, she leaned back and he kissed her.

He paid attention to her, just as he had to the statues. Amy knew he'd never kissed another woman exactly this way, smiling into her lips and tugging gently on the hair at the nape of her neck, slowly settling his body tighter against hers, breath by breath.

"I've wanted to do that since the moment I saw you on the bus," Paul said.

"Yeah?" Amy grinned, becoming a beautiful woman in her memory of the previous day.

He kissed her once more, quickly, like he was grabbing one last bite of something delicious. "It's not all I've been wanting." The pressure of his hands on her arms changed. His words hung in the air between them.

Amy blinked and found her new boldness could take her no further. She did not want to become a travel cliché: eating, praying, and getting laid. She dotted an ellipsis of kisses across the line of his jaw. "Let's go inside," she said, and they did. Their hands remained linked, but Paul did not kiss Amy again.

They went sightseeing together every day, until Amy realized that the next day would be her last in Hong Kong. Instead of parting with him at the subway station, she lingered. Paul asked if she wanted to eat together at a noodle shop and she agreed.

Across from Paul in the crowded, smoky restaurant, Amy's sense of ease with him slipped. She kept thinking about the airplane she'd be on the day after tomorrow, speculating at what exact moment the joy and freedom she had found would slip away. Paul had three days longer in Hong Kong than she did, and she wondered if he would simply find another woman to go with him on his pilgrimage.

"Where do you want to go tomorrow?" Paul asked.

She didn't want to go anywhere. She wanted to know what it would be like to lie in his arms. This was how the cliché got started, Amy thought. Less than forty-eight hours until her plane back to everyday life, she would try anything to hold on to what she'd found here, even if that meant squandering the opportunity of being in a foreign country by spending the rest of her time there making love to a man who lived a five-hour drive from her house.

She met his eyes. She could not speak.

"There's nothing you want to see?" Paul leaned in, encouraging her.

Amy took a deep breath and went for his mouth. "There is," she gasped, after they narrowly escaped knocking over their noodle bowls in the course of their wild kiss.

Amy had never been so forward before, and her hands trembled. When Paul let them into his hotel room, she hugged him and used this as a chance to hide her face a minute. She tried to calm down. When she met his gaze again, his face reflected the same wonder and excitement she'd seen at the statue.

"I guess everybody does this," Amy said, grasping for reality.

Paul grinned. "Not everybody has a Jacuzzi in their room." He picked her up and swung her in his arms. She shrieked and laughed in relief. Sex had been urgent before, but she had never thought of it as fun.

They played like children, undressing each other and giggling and screaming when the Jacuzzi water ran too hot. They splashed all over the bathroom. She pulled his hands to her breasts and made out with him like it was her first time, clumsy and happy.

Amy kissed Paul, then stuck out her tongue and tickled the underside of his cock. "Oh, you're going to play it like that," said Paul. He dipped his head under the water and blew bubbles against her clit. Amy squealed and slapped at him, but he wrapped his arms around her thighs to hold her in place. His tongue lapped against her along with the bubbles, and Amy stopped struggling. She let him continue a moment longer before pulling his head up by the hair. "I want you," she said.

"Are you sure?"

She rolled her eyes at the tease in his voice, and wrapped her legs around his waist. "Believe me. I'm sure."

"I don't think so," Paul said. "I think what you really want is this." He spun her suddenly, positioning her so the Jacuzzi jet fountained right against her clit.

Amy jerked in his grasp. "When you put it that way..." Pleasant tension gathered between her thighs.

"Tell you what," Paul said. A condom wrapper tore open behind her. "How about I give you both?" His cock pressed against her from behind while the water continued to massage her clit. She had stopped giggling by then. He felt too good. She rolled her clit back and forth across the water stream while he rocked in and out of her. She turned back to catch his mouth. The kiss went on forever, his tongue hot but patient against hers. She climbed slowly toward her pleasure, with Paul her companion, just as he had been on the steps up to the monastery. When she finally gasped into his mouth and began to shudder, she felt his grin against her shoulder.

They didn't even go outside the next day, spending every moment connected—skin to skin, tongue to tongue, his body inside hers. Before falling asleep on her last night in Hong Kong, Amy let Paul cradle her in his lap. "It would just hurt, wouldn't it?" she whispered. "Trying to keep this?"

"Says who?"

She stared at him. His face seemed earnest, intent and incredibly familiar considering how short a time she had known him. "That's the way the stories always go. This is just a fling, right? I should accept that and not ruin it?" But Amy spoke in questions rather than declaratives. She wanted Paul to prove her wrong.

"We don't have to listen to the stories," he said. He tilted her chin up to his, their lips meeting softly then pressing harder together. "Can't we be like this in Florida? Visit places together? Have fun with each other?"

When he put it that way, Amy didn't see why they couldn't. Looking at Paul, she didn't see why the joy, freedom and wonder they'd felt together had to fade at all. She flung her arms around him and dragged him back toward the Jacuzzi.

THE "TILLY" CROWN AFFAIR

Michael M. Jones

Ever since she first watched Rene Russo, playing a confidently sexy insurance investigator, stalk onscreen and proceed to own every scene she was in, Tilly has been obsessed with *The Thomas Crown Affair*. (Not the original, but the 1999 version that starred Pierce Brosnan in the titular role.) She nursed a heavy crush on Russo's character for years, enjoying lusty fantasies about long legs, red hair, pale skin, and that pin-striped skirt-and-jacket outfit. With scenes from the movie playing in her mind, she spread her legs and touched herself, fingers slipping between her thighs to touch, to tease, to satisfy. In her mind, it was "Tilly" Crown matching wits with the bold-as-brass Catherine Banning, dancing with her, seducing her. For years, it was Tilly's go-to fantasy, the one that left her wet and panting, satiated and purring. For years, it was as close as she'd ever get to realizing her crush. But then she met Charlene, who loved movies just as much as she did...and together they pondered ways to make it work.

It took several viewings of the movie—oft-paused and rewound due to more personal distractions—for the two women to nail down the scene that absolutely, positively, undeniably worked for them. Not so coincidentally, it was that one scene, involving Russo in a semitransparent black dress, featuring a whole lot of dirty dancing, which proved the most distracting. The remote was lost behind the cushions as Tilly ended up with a lapful of Charlene, the lithe blonde making herself quite at home against Tilly's generous curves and warm skin. With lips meeting and hands in motion, it was quite a while before they were able to backtrack and pick up where they'd left off. It only took two words for them to agree on a plan. "That scene," whispered Tilly, nipping at Charlene's ear. "That scene, and I'm yours for life."

It took some effort to make it actually happen, of course. One simply doesn't find a high-class black-and-white-dress ball just anywhere, not even if you're looking. One doesn't simply waltz in, either. Not unless one has an invitation—or friends in interesting places. Luckily, they had the latter; a friend of a friend who worked as a caterer for high-society functions and who could maybe look the other way by the back door for a minute. It was a mixture of cunning and luck, audacity and erotic ambition. With Tilly's words still haunting her memories, Charlene was ready to move heaven and earth to fulfill this request.

The stage was set. Tilly entered first, almost but not quite blending in with her tuxedo—sans tie, just like the movie— curves bound, short dark hair slicked down. She'd never have passed for Pierce Brosnan, but with a bit of a swagger she certainly confused some of the onlookers. Those who even noticed, of course. She found a dance partner, a pretty blonde woman temporarily abandoned by her date and tipsy on expensive champagne, and sweet-talked her into a dance.

A few minutes later, as the Afro-Cuban band playing in the background changed numbers, Charlene made her appearance. She'd tucked her blonde hair up under a bold red wig, wriggled into "the dress," the sleek, semitransparent number that sparkled and shone against the lights, and draped a red wrap over her shoulders. Charlene was almost two decades too young to play Rene Russo—devilishly sexy at forty-five when the movie came out—but she made up for it in confidence and style. Tight nipples poked at the dress, eye-catching whenever the light hit it just so. She shimmied as she walked, stalking toward Tilly and her dance partner. Heads turned to follow her, the eyes of men and women alike following the sashay of her ass, accompanied by mumbles as they tried to place her. That hotel heiress? The ex-teenybopper actress? She had to be someone.

Tilly and Charlene met, their eyes locked, an erotic charge leaping between them. Tilly's heart pounded as she embraced the role of "Tilly" Crown, facing off against "Charlene" Banning. The memories of a hundred hot masturbation sessions with her vibrator buzzing at her clit and her pussy soaked with arousal rushed in, and the heat rose between her legs. Charlene tapped the blonde on the shoulder, capturing her attention as well. "I'm cutting in," she announced.

The blonde blinked, but Tilly smiled apologetically, kissed her on the cheek and sent her on her way. Another night, another set of circumstances, and Tilly and Charlene might have kept their new friend, drawn her into their games if she was willing—and a gut instinct told Tilly that was possible—but this was not that night, nor those circumstances. "It's a black-and-white ball," replied Tilly, giving Charlene her cockiest grin. They knew the lines, had them down pat, recited them without missing a beat.

"I wasn't invited anyway," Charlene shot back, and they

moved into each other's arms, coming together in a slow dance, an elegant set of moves mirroring the crowd around them. They bantered back and forth, each word carrying an erotic, electric charge. Charlene's fair skin was flushed with desire, telltale red creeping down the deep-cut neckline. Tilly's arousal grew, her pussy damp with anticipation. They followed their script, and then, with perfect timing, the band followed theirs. A little extra money, a private plea to make this night memorable, and the musicians had happily gone along with the chance to spice things up. They switched from a slow song into a fast, sexy, sensual beat, and things got...interesting.

Charlene was bold and provocative, Tilly confident and dominant, and they danced like they planned to fuck, taunting and teasing each other. The dress flashed and sparkled, the thin fabric showing off hard nipples and bare skin underneath, broken only by the lines of a tiny black thong. Charlene spun, showing off the curves of her ass, brazen and blatant. Tilly caught her, drew her in, spun her out, reeled her back in. They exchanged fierce looks, stalking each other at arms' length. They came together, Charlene grinding her body against Tilly's, the dress and tuxedo barely there against their combined heat.

And then they were face-to-face once again, Charlene's eyes hooded in a sultry, come-hither expression that almost had Tilly on her knees, until she remembered that she was "Tilly" Crown and this was her moment. "Do you want to dance?" she asked, voice low and throaty, "or do you want to *dance*?"

Their mouths crashed together in a hungry kiss, lips parting, tongues dancing, chests heaving, hands moving slowly over fabric. All around them, people stopped to stare and mutter— some with envy, others with dismay.

By the time they were escorted out of the building, they were laughing. Arm-in-arm, they stumbled down the stairs and outside into the night. There was no way they could go home, not to the old and familiar on a night like this, so they'd made reservations at a certain nearby hotel, somewhere classy but not exorbitant. "I'm not doing it on the marble floor or the stairs," Charlene had declared during the initial discussions. "That's just hell on the back."

So with kisses and touches to keep the spark alive, they hailed a cab for the short ride over, careful not to give the cabbie *too* much of a show—though as Charlene's dress hiked up and Tilly's buttons came undone, it was a hard thing to prevent—and eventually made it to their room.

The door hadn't even fully shut before Tilly had Charlene pressed up against the wall, kissing her with a desperate hunger. She tugged at the dress's thin straps, pulling them down over Charlene's shoulders, and it slowly puddled to the floor, leaving the woman in nothing but the tiny black thong—soaked through with need—and matching high heels. The rest of her was bare: pale skin thoroughly flushed, nipples hard, ready and aching to be fulfilled.

Tilly slipped her hand between Charlene's legs, tugging the thong aside, and found her pussy slick and ready. She pushed several fingers into Charlene, fucking her in long, quick strokes, kissing her in time to the motions. She swallowed Charlene's gasps, devoured her cries of ecstasy and reveled in the quick, inevitable orgasm. She held her lover close as she shuddered and whimpered, and knew that while Rene Russo had been a fabulous fantasy, she'd found a reality that was far, far better.

The two finished undressing, and took each other to bed, where "Tilly" Crown and "Charlene" Banning ravished each other until they were sweaty, exhausted and satiated.

Charlene stretched out, sighing in happy contentment as Tilly draped herself against her. "You remember how I said that if you gave me that scene, I was yours for life?" Tilly murmured.

Charlene's lips curled into a lazy smile. "I could never forget."

"I meant it. Marry me."

Charlene's answer was almost immediate. "Absolutely. Have I ever told you about my favorite movie wedding?"

GENTLE
TEASING

Raelynn MacDonald

D evon reclined on the bed in Sarah's apartment, a smile
tugging at his lips as he idly ran his hands over the bedspread
beneath him. His senses were rapidly becoming clouded by the
faint scent of perfume that hung in the air and thoughts of Sarah
while he waited for her. The soft sound of a throat clearing
caused him to turn his head, his half-closed eyes opening fully
at the sight that greeted him.

Sitting up, he stared at Sarah, framed in the doorway, with
an expression at once lustful and loving. Her hair was piled in
a messy bun at the back of her head, with thin strands hanging
down in tendrils to frame her face, and her hazel eyes shone
with a smile as she looked back at him. Taking in the rest of
her appearance, it was all Devon could do to keep himself from
gaping at her. Slowly, Sarah sauntered across the room toward
him, her tight, knee-length negligee clinging to the curve of her
hips as she moved.

"Sarah," Devon whispered, as Sarah leaned close to brush

their lips together; when she pulled back, she looked at him through half-lidded eyes. Devon's own eyes were immediately drawn to the bow of Sarah's lips as her tongue darted across them, and he leaned in to close the gap between them once again. Tilting her head to deepen the kiss, Sarah knelt up onto the bed to straddle Devon's lap and slipped her hands beneath his shirt to caress his bare skin.

Devon moved his hands to grip Sarah's waist and attempted to pull her closer, only to be stopped when she pulled back with a soft laugh. Her glance was smoldering as she deftly unbuttoned his shirt, pushing the fabric from his shoulders and tossing it to the floor. With a gentle nudge of her hand, he lay back on the bed and Sarah bent over him. Her lips trailed kisses down from his neck to his chest, while her hands reached down to begin working at opening his pants.

When he began pulling at the straps of her lingerie a moment later, Sarah sat back to bat his hands away. "Now, now," she admonished, wagging a finger at him. "None of that just yet." Devon's brow furrowed, but Sarah continued before he could ask why she was stopping him. "I have something planned for you."

There was a mischievous glint in her eyes as she winked at him, standing up from the bed and crossing the room to her dresser. Devon rolled onto his side, watching the slight sway of Sarah's hips as she walked, too distracted to notice the object she removed from the drawer until she turned. Sarah separated the small bundle of black silk into four strips as she approached the bed again, laying them out on the mattress.

Realizing what she was up to, Devon allowed Sarah to divest him of the rest of his clothing before stretching himself out on the bed. He reached his arms and legs out toward the corners of the head- and footboards and watched as Sarah's lips twitched in amusement. He held himself still while she tied him, and once her task was completed, Sarah stepped back to survey her handiwork.

Light bondage was not uncommon between them, but until tonight, it had always been Sarah on the receiving end of the activity. As she looked him over now, Devon watched a thrill ripple through her body as her eyes raked over him spread naked on her bed. Crawling back over him, she resumed her previous position straddling his waist and leaned down to capture his lips in another kiss. Devon's lips parted beneath hers with a moan as Sara slipped a hand between them to close her slender fingers around his erection, just a moment before she pulled back with a sultry smile and then bent to trail kisses down over his body once again.

His eyes followed her movements as she neared the base of his cock and her tongue darted out to lick a stripe along the underside of his shaft. Rolling his hips in an attempt to gain more of her attention, he tipped his head back with a loud gasp when she complied and closed her mouth over him to suck softly. Her tongue swirled around the sensitive head, and for several moments, she tortured him with her delicate ministrations, her hands gently pressed against his hips to keep him from bucking up into her mouth.

When she released him from between her lips, Devon let out a groan of protest and opened his eyes to look at her, only to find Sarah smiling as she began to crawl her way back up along his body. She pressed her lips to the corner of his mouth, pulling away when he strained upward to kiss her more firmly and instead, moved out of his reach to stretch out beside him. She supported her head on one hand and stroked the other over his chest and down, bypassing his erection in favor of teasing her fingers against his thigh.

"Please," he finally gasped, arching into her caresses.

She laughed softly in response and sat up to place herself in his lap again. Taking hold of the hem of her negligee, she slowly slid the fabric up over her body while he watched, his eyes relishing every inch of her exposed flesh.

"You want me to untie you already?" Sarah's lips quirked up in a smile as she let the piece of lingerie slip from her fingers to fall to the floor.

Devon's heart pounded as he raked his gaze over the gentle swell of her breasts and down over her flat stomach to the scrap of black lace panties she still wore. Momentarily forgetting what he'd been asked, he murmured, "God, I want you..."

Sarah leaned over him to release his hands, and hardly had the chance to straighten before he sat up and wrapped an arm around her waist, pulling her against his chest. His free hand curled around the back of her neck as he kissed her, parting his lips and darting his tongue out to swipe across her lower lip. When her lips parted in answer, he took the invitation to deepen the kiss, drawing a soft moan from her.

When they broke apart, Sarah's eyes were fluttering and her cheeks flushed as she panted softly for breath. After giving her a gentle reminder of his restrained ankles, he waited for her to release them before pushing her down onto her back. With one hand, he gathered her wrists and pinned them above her head as he leaned down and kissed along the curve of her neck. Devon's other hand glided down between her legs, feeling the damp fabric there and chuckling.

"I see I'm not the only one who was being teased, then."

Devon's fingers found the thin strings at Sarah's hips that held her panties in place and tugged, allowing the fabric to fall open. The soft gasp that left her lips then was quickly followed by a moan as his fingers found her clit.

"You look so beautiful," he murmured in her ear as she

rocked her hips beneath his touch, receiving a whimper from her in response.

"Please, baby..."

Drawing his hand away, he positioned himself between her legs and slid slowly into her wet heat. He felt her body stiffen briefly before she relaxed with a soft sigh of pleasure. He returned his hand to her clit, rubbing against it as he began to move in and out of her eager body. Once again, Sarah writhed against him, silently begging for more; her hips rolled up to meet his thrusts, allowing her to take him deeper as he increased his speed. Leaning down, he buried his face against her neck, kissing and nipping at her skin as her moans filled his ears.

Before long, he felt her body quivering beneath him, just before her muscles contracted around him and her back arched beautifully as her orgasm wracked her body. The sensation of her coming around him drove him to his own completion a moment later, and he brought their lips together one last time as he moaned his release.

They lay together as they came down from their orgasm, both breathing heavily, until Devon moved to stretch out beside Sarah. She rolled to face him, and he gently pushed a strand of hair from her beautiful face. His simple gesture brought a smile to her lips as she cuddled closer to him, and he wrapped his arms around her, lightly stroking her hair as he placed a kiss against the top of her head.

EIGHTY
CUPCAKES

Neve Black

It started with a phone call.

"Sure, I can bring cupcakes. No problem—I'm going to bake them myself," I answered confidently.

There was a long moment of silence, then my sister asked, "You're sure you want to *make* them?"

I responded as cheerfully as possible. "Yes, I'm sure I want to *make* them. It's not a problem, really. Jacob will help me."

"Costco has great cupcakes."

"That's nice. I'm going to make eighty cupcakes for Mom's birthday party," I volleyed. I was not backing down.

"Okay, I'll see you then. Love you. Bye," she reluctantly acquiesced, while hurrying me off the phone.

"Okay, bye." I squeaked my response before the phone went silent.

Eighty cupcakes. No problem.

My mom's eightieth birthday fell on a very hot Saturday in July. My boyfriend Jacob and I woke early that day, made love and then ran a few miles before the sun started its attack on the day. We had most of the latter part of the morning to devote to the cupcake baking and decorating challenge before the birthday festivities started that afternoon.

It's important that I mention my relationship with Jacob was still new at the time—we had been dating for just six months and were newly in love. We were steadfastly in the honeymoon stage, which as everyone knows is often filled with giddy infatuation. Part of our giddiness factor was what I affectionately referred to as the stare-down: the long, lustful gazes we'd steal of each other while in the midst of various, mundane tasks. These wanton-romantic stare-downs would lead to kissing and groping, which led to wet panties and one very hard cock. This of course would lead to clothes coming off, more groping and kissing and then, ultimately, the two of us fucking like a couple of wild animals. Suffice to say, we couldn't get enough of each other. And yet, I still planned to make eighty cupcakes for Mom's birthday.

With the day stretched out before us, we needed to hit the grocery store to purchase necessary cupcake-baking items. After a shower, I slipped into a navy-blue tank top, a short skirt and flip-flops. I was commando from head to silver toe ring. Climbing into Jacob's Mercedes, I found that the dark-tinted windows kept the black leather cool and it felt good against my warm skin. His familiar strong, tanned hand reached for my upper thigh and gave me a tender squeeze. I pushed my damp hair against the headrest and he moved in and kissed me.

"Baby, we need to get going. We have a lot of baking to do," he whispered after a long, heated moment.

"You're a tease."

When I stepped inside the store, the chilly air made my nipples hard and visible through my tank top. I crossed my sun-kissed arms over my breasts, trying to hide them from Jacob. I didn't want to give him any excuse to fondle me. We had cupcakes to bake. In the baking aisle perusing flour and sugar, I pushed a strand of wavy hair away from my face as I glanced across the aisle at Jacob. I smiled at him. His suntanned skin looked shimmery in the fluorescent lights. I admired his athletic build—flat stomach, muscle-toned legs, arms and chest. And I also noticed his nipples had hardened from the crisp, air-conditioned store, just like mine. He looked so sexy standing there sorting through the baking spices and extracts. The lines crinkled seductively around his blue eyes as he smiled back at me. He glanced down at my breasts and I felt an inevitable staredown in our near future.

I had to force myself to focus on cupcakes and not on the prospect of getting naked with Jacob. Again. We needed to hustle if we were going to get to the party on time with eighty freshly baked and frosted cupcakes. I turned away from him quickly and pushed the cart toward the dairy department. Jacob followed suit. His body eclipsed mine from behind as his muscular chest pushed up against my back. His hands covered mine and the hairs on his legs tickled my thighs. He smelled fresh and soapy-clean and the cool, damp tips of his dark hair brushed against my cheek. I could feel his hardening cock through his shorts as he continued to push up against me. I closed my eyes, fighting the urge to turn around and kiss him right in the middle of the grocery store. I felt my pussy tighten. I was getting wet.

"Baby, what are you doing? Your sexiness is seriously distracting me," I said softly, conscious of people around us.

"I couldn't help but notice that you're cold, so I'm warming you up."

We reached the dairy section and Jacob unwrapped his sexy

body from mine. He grabbed a can of whipping cream and tossed it into the cart. "That's for later," he said casually.

I felt my clit start to throb. Weak kneed, I tried to focus on the task at hand as I reached for eggs, milk and butter.

Finally, I took inventory of the contents in the grocery cart. "I think we're all set, sweetie."

"Great, let's get going then. If we hurry, your nipples will still be hard when we get to the car—I really want to suck on them."

He was relentless and I was helpless against his determination. The very thought of his lips and tongue smothering my nipples nearly made me come right there, standing between the sour cream and the yogurt. I was slippery wet and I was undeniably hungry for him. I started to think that maybe we should have just bought the damn cupcakes because clearly the baking process was going to be delayed.

He smiled at me and kept raising his eyebrows up and down while we waited in line at the checkout. I was fidgety and distracted, unbelievably horny. You wouldn't have thought we had just had sex a few hours ago. All I wanted to do was get out of there—and go back to his house and have more sex. I was a certifiable sex fiend with him, and I couldn't seem to get enough.

Sliding into the car, I looked over at Jacob and he looked over at me with that knowing, sexy smirk. The stare-down had escalated—and I knew we wouldn't make it home. He unzipped his pants and pulled out his hard cock, already glistening with precome. Then he began stroking himself while staring at me.

A girl can only take so much. Moving quickly, and not really caring about where we were, I awkwardly crawled over the middle console and onto Jacob's lap. Straddling him, I pulled my skirt up and over my hips, while Jacob pushed his seat back.

We started kissing with the kind of intense passion we always shared. I lifted myself up and onto his cock and felt the head pierce my pussy's opening as I slid down, his hardness going deeper inside of me. God, it felt so good.

I was moaning and moving up and down on him, the right side of my knee jammed between the car seat and the door. It hurt, but it was a good kind of hurt. It added to the excitement. I didn't care if anyone saw us either, but for the most part we were hidden behind the dark-tinted windows. Jacob's hands were on my hips, helping me move up and down on his cock. I felt his hand move up under my tank top, pulling it up so his lips could suck my nipple, as he promised he would do. I moaned louder. His cock rubbed against my clit, massaging and teasing me without mercy. I was getting close to coming already—riding him like that in a public place, cocooned from the heat in his car—all of it felt extraordinary.

Jacob was getting close too. His cock was harder than ever.

"I'm going to come, baby," I breathed with a shuddery whisper.

"Come. Come all over me, you fire-cat...I'm right behind you."

Jacob rolled his tongue around and around and back and forth across my aching nipple as he pulled my hips down onto him harder and faster. My clit exploded and all of the lusty buildup was released, sending sweet spasms of orgasmic pleasure over me.

My orgasm spurred Jacob to come, too. "Oh, baby...now." He pressed his head against my breasts.

When our orgasms had subsided, the reality of where we were and what we'd been doing quickly set in. I dislodged my battered knee and moved off of Jacob, carefully finding my way back into the passenger seat. Jacob zipped up his shorts and started the engine. We giggled all the way home. As we reached his house, an unspoken pact was established between us: no more stare-downs until the cupcake project was complete. Later that afternoon, we somehow managed to arrive at the party with eighty freshly baked and decorated birthday cupcakes. Our car tryst had only set us back about thirty minutes.

"Carla, these cupcakes are really good," my sister called from across the room.

"Thank you," I said, feeling triumphant in my success and still glowing from my sexual conquest.

Jacob was devouring a chocolate cupcake and he winked at me enticingly. "Not bad, babe."

I smiled and winked back before saying, "Mmm...whipping cream."

And just like that, our stare-down was back on.

COMPANY PICNIC

Anya M. Wassenberg

The sweat pours from my forehead down my chin—the heat of the grill, I tell myself. I watch him under my lashes as he gets closer and closer. A bit of fat liquefies, drips from a hamburger and sizzles in ecstasy as it hits the flame. I drop my eyes back down to the barbecue even as I hear his footsteps coming closer over the concrete of the pavilion floor.

"Ready for a break, Grumpy? I need an excuse to stay out of the three-legged race," he laughs, that rich, dark laugh. I feel a pang—it's been so long; I have no defenses when he's this close and when he's this beautiful.

Grumpy looks up like he didn't know who was coming. He hesitates a second, and a flicker of an expression flits across his face. He looks over at me quickly—it seems long but maybe it's my imagination. "Sure. Thanks Byron."

"Thanks, I can use the help," I say stiffly, my eyes still turned downward. "I hear you're doing really well out West."

"I guess I am."

"I was beginning to think you weren't going to come over to say hello at all."

He stares at me for a second with the big eyes I still find myself daydreaming about in weaker moments. "Marie, you're the only reason I came here today."

"But you didn't even know I was coming!" I scoff, and it feels good to get a little distance from those eyes and the slant of his cheekbones. "I didn't know I was coming myself until—"

"Until Daphne called you to tell you she hurt her back, and could you help Grumpy with the grill," he says, and a smile curls at the corners of his mouth, one that my body remembers with a rush of desire that startles me.

I frown. "What...?"

"Daphne is my mother's second cousin; I guess you didn't really know that," he says, his mouth now stretched into a grin. "I've known her all my life."

"But..."

"I didn't think you'd see me otherwise. I thought you'd pull that *I'm doing what's good for you* shit again."

I turn another hot dog and then stop. Wait just a second here. "But it *was* good for you. Do you honestly think they would have promoted you here if the powers that be knew about us? And besides..."

"Besides what? I should be with some nice, young *black* girl?"

I look around quickly to give myself some breathing room. What the hell is happening here? He can't just come back here and... My eyes scan quickly but no one seems to be looking over. Ardene and her crew are busy organizing the wheelbarrow race on the lawn. Grumpy sits a few tables away. He turns briefly and raises his can of pop in a salute.

"I thought you were engaged."

"Ramona was no fool. She knew, she could tell."

"Tell what?"

So open and deep, his eyes stare into me from above his full lips. "You're the only one on my mind."

"Oh my god." It's all I can think of to say. The smell of burning hot dogs assaults my nose. "Jesus!"

Byron laughs and it makes my insides shiver, but for the next few minutes we busy ourselves saving the hot dogs from a blackened fate. It's a few minutes before order is restored.

"I came back for you," he says, "I'm leaving Westcliff and setting up my own shop. I want you to come out West, come be my partner."

"In business?" I ask incredulously.

"In business and in my bed," he insists. His voice is low but steady.

I can't help my response, the immediate tug on my middle. It takes me back to that very first day when Doug in accounting came around to introduce his new protégé, that moment when I first saw his face.

"Nobody knows yet? That you're leaving Westcliff?" I begin to turn the row of hamburgers on the upper rack one by one, making myself concentrate as the idea sinks in.

"Just you and my Auntie Daphne." His voice pauses and I look up, spatula in hand, to see him staring at me.

And just as my brain becomes seized, paralyzed by the thoughts that swirl around too quickly, hope begins to bubble in my gut. A few moments pass where the only sound is the sizzling on the grill. We move in tandem to deal with the hamburgers and hot dogs in succession, turning, flipping.

"You know, I remember documenting the fact that your reports tended to lack detail," I say and begin to laugh.

He joins in. There are lines at the side of his mouth as he

laughs louder; I watch the movement of muscle underneath his dark chocolate skin. Something deep and potent reaches up from memory, and I'm lost for a moment. Byron is still talking, small talk now as a group from the social committee makes its way to the salad table next to us. I don't follow his words, staring at the dirty concrete floor of the pavilion and lost now in the memory of the *last* time I saw him, his last day in our office.

It was January, bitter cold. He was packing things in boxes and I went to his office in the morning—we were always there before anyone else. His window up on the eleventh floor looked way down to the street. Above there were thin white clouds, far, far up, and big fat flakes of snow that drifted down in a graceful dance around the building, swirling around just in front of the glass. I stood in the doorway for what seemed like a very long while just watching him before he noticed I was there. He said nothing, just held out his hand, and smiled *that* smile, that look that was just for me, and I closed the door behind me before moving toward him.

His kiss, that's what drew me in from the very first time, so soft, barely touching my lips, like he didn't want to miss a single taste. His fingertips brushing my face and my neck before passing down my body to reach under my skirt and between my legs. Just the memory of it now on this sunlit afternoon makes me wet, heating me from the inside. I shiver slightly at the intensity of it and stare at him while he tends to the grill. People must be talking. I see Ardene whispering with Kathleen as they fuss with salads, but I sink back into the memory the same way I could never keep myself away from him.

I began to unbutton his shirt, first slowly, then he took over, impatient, and we stripped each other hurriedly, giggling, uncontrollable. If I close my eyes I can see his chest, his muscled body, and reach for it again like I did that day.

"You make me so hard," he whispers, "and I know you still want me, no matter what you say."

I make him sit on the desk so I can kiss him, lick him down to his belly and then take him in my mouth just to hear the sounds he makes, just to hear him sigh and know that I did it. Then he pulls me up and we kiss, and I'm so lost in him, so lost. He leads me to a chair and kneels in front and slowly makes me come with his warm, wet tongue. I kiss him just to taste myself.

I'm on his desk, on top of our clothes with my thighs wide apart. He enters me and there's only our slippery friction and ragged breaths; he likes to make it last longer, pushing slowly all the way in and then out, keeping me at arm's length instead of falling on me so I'm enveloped in this impossible high. I never got enough of him, could never get enough. I arch myself toward him, pushing my head back to open my eyes and there's only the blue, blue sky, and the waltzing flakes of snow from upside down, conscious of memorizing the moment, how this feels, *how fucking incredible this feels*—everything...

"Say you'll at least have dinner with me, let me fill in my proposal with a few more details?" he asks. His words come more quickly, urgently. "You can't tell me this is what you really want—walking on eggshells all the time, dealing with office politics and race politics all rolled up into one. Come West with me. We'll make our own rules."

I open my eyes now to the park, the company picnic, frozen in the present. Voices chatter and the grill sizzles. Then I turn to find Byron and he's staring back at me, into my wide-open eyes.

"Say you will," he insists.

But all I can do is smile.

IMAGINATION
AT PLAY

Brighton Walsh

The spark of a fantasy had been forming in my head since we'd gotten home from the bar. The problem was I wasn't exactly sure how to put it in action. My boyfriend and I had always been open with each other about our fantasies and had tried a handful of the things we'd talked about. The idea of a threesome had been something that he'd told me he fantasized about, but it was never something either of us would act on, unsure of how it would affect our relationship.

Even though he would never bring another person home with us, he still appreciated the opposite sex as much as the next guy, and I noticed when his eyes lingered on a beautiful woman, even as subtle as he was.

That night, his eyes had lingered a lot.

Erik was sprawled on the couch, his head resting against the top of the cushions. I went to him and climbed onto his lap, straddling his hips. His cock wasn't yet hard, but I knew that it wouldn't take much. As I slowly rocked over him, his hands found my hips, lightly encouraging me, and he hummed his approval. A smile curved the corners of his lips, and I leaned forward to trace my tongue along them.

I rained kisses along his jaw and up to his ear. I nibbled and licked, just how I knew he liked, and when I finally found my nerve, I said, "I saw you watching her."

He stilled under me, his body going stiff. "Who?"

"You know who. The blonde at the bar, legs a mile long, boobs pushed up to her chin, lips to die for...ringing any bells?"

"Jenna," he said softly, hesitantly, almost as if he wasn't sure if he was in trouble or not.

"I'm not mad," I reassured him as my hands made their familiar path along his shoulders and chest to the waistband of his jeans. "I noticed her, too."

His hands regained their actions, gently rocking me along his growing erection. He reached back and cupped my ass, tilting his head so he could place kisses along my neck.

With my mouth still at his ear, I whispered, "What would you do if she was here with us?"

"Jesus, Jen, what are you doing to me?"

I pulled back and looked him in the eye. Playing with the hair at the nape of his neck, I leaned forward and nipped his lips. "We said we'd never bring anyone else to bed with us, but that doesn't mean you can't have your fantasy. Now, tell me, when you think about it, what happens? What is she doing with us?"

I continued kissing him, but he remained silent. I knew he was probably hesitant to say anything, afraid of overstepping the boundaries that had only just become blurry.

Knowing that I had to get it started, I asked, "Does she watch us? Maybe while she fingers herself? Or is she part of the action? Does she go down on you while I watch? Or maybe she goes down on *me*..."

"Christ," he groaned, and I knew I had hit the jackpot with the last scenario.

We were both still dressed, so I ran my hands over the ridges of muscles on his abdomen and chest, lifting his shirt as I went. I pulled it off, doing the same with mine, then reached down and released him from his jeans, his cock thick and hard in my hand. He freed me of my bra, his breathing rapid as I stroked his impressive length, running my thumb over the head and spreading the moisture I found there.

When he remained silent, I leaned forward, breathing more life into his fantasy. "What are you doing while she licks my pussy? Are you sitting back and watching, jerking off? Come on, baby, tell me."

"*Fuck*." I could tell the minute his control snapped because he stood with me still wrapped around him, set me on my feet, and stripped my jeans and panties from me. He spun me around so my back was pressed against his front then guided me until I was on my knees at his feet. Following me down, he pressed his thighs to the back of mine and arched over me. With his lips pressed to my ear, he said, "You want to know what I'm doing? I'm enjoying the view, because it's not just her licking your pussy, but you've got your face buried in hers, too."

I moaned, my back arching as I reached back to hook my arm around his neck. Turning my head, I met his frantic kiss, his hands gripping my breasts harshly, his fingers twisting my nipples until I cried out. Sliding one hand down my body, he found my pussy and slid his fingers along my slit.

"Jesus, Jenna, you're wet. This turns you on, too, doesn't it? Thinking about eating her pussy while I watch."

I couldn't find words to answer as he slipped two fingers

inside me, his palm grinding against my clit as he fucked me with his fingers. He kissed along my shoulder, teeth scraping as he went. With a final brush of his lips, he removed his fingers from my body and pressed his hand between my shoulder blades, bending me forward until I was on my hands and knees. I heard rustling, the ripping of a condom packet and then felt him against me again, his panting breaths sweeping across the side of my face as I felt his cock nudge my pussy.

"Do you know what happens then, baby?" His voice was like honey over gravel, all rough and sticky sweet. "When she's got you so close to coming with her tongue that you're begging for it, I fuck you." He flexed his hips, entering me in one thrust while he brushed his fingers back and forth over my clit. "Just like this, pounding into you from behind while she licks and sucks your clit."

"Oh god, Erik." I turned my head back to him, blindly searching for his mouth while he fucked me hard.

He slammed into me over and over, his frantic rhythm telling me just how worked up this had gotten him. His mouth met mine, clumsy and urgent as he kept his pace.

He was bent over me, one hand strumming my clit while the other pinched and pulled at my nipples. With the fantasy still vibrant in my mind, it wasn't long before I found my release, my pussy squeezing his cock as I pulsed through my climax.

"Oh fuck, yeah," he groaned, his open mouth pressing against my shoulder as his thrusts turned erratic. He grunted and filled me completely as he came.

Spent and sated, my legs feeling like jelly, I collapsed on the floor, relishing his comforting weight on top of me.

"Wow." His voice was muffled against my skin.

"Good 'wow'?" I asked, the pangs of nervousness encroaching.

He chuckled, throaty and low. "Fucking great 'wow.' But maybe next time you warn me before springing something like that on me."

I turned my head, meeting his lips, and grinned. "Now where's the fun in that?"

HEIGHTEN
THE SENSES

Heidi Champa

I lie on the bed, my naked body against the cool, crisp sheets. The collar around my neck sports a chain that keeps me tethered to the headboard. I can move my head, but only when you want me to. My feet are equally trapped, each ankle strapped snuggly to a bedpost. My thighs are splayed wide; my pussy is already aching and wet. My hands are blissfully free, but only because you allow it—command it. I start running my hands down my chest like I'm told, stopping to tweak each nipple, twisting and squeezing until the peaks are hard and swollen with blood. My mouth opens, moans escaping my lips. Just like you want. Always like you want.

"Pinch those nipples harder. I really want to hear you."

I do as I am told, inflicting pain on myself just to please you. I moan louder as I ride the cresting wave of pain and pleasure. My pussy tightens, a fresh wash of moisture clings to my swollen lips. I hear you sigh with satisfaction. I cast a glance your way, but your face is impassive. Just like it always is when we play your games.

"That's it. Good girl. Now, keep those hands moving."

My hands continue their downward journey, a small giggle bubbling up when I graze my sensitive hip bone. You register that sound too.

"I love that you are so ticklish, even when you touch yourself. But keep going, I didn't tell you to stop."

"Yes, Sir."

I barely croak out the words and I hear your agitation.

"Say it like you mean it, or this whole thing stops. And you don't want that, do you?"

"No, Sir. I'm sorry, Sir. Please, forgive me, Sir."

I'm already begging. I hope you can hear it and that it pleases you. You pause for interminable seconds. When you finally speak, you seem satisfied. For now.

"Keep going, my little slut. I want you to spread that cunt open and play with yourself for me."

My breathing is hard and fast when I get to my wet pussy. I hesitate, pausing to catch my breath before I gently ease my cunt lips apart. The room is silent with anticipation, until I rub a finger over the hard nub of my clit. My cries fill the room, bouncing back to my ears in a thick echo. I keep going, two fingers now sliding over and around my hot button. My throaty moans are getting louder, but it is your voice I want to hear. I crave your approval and can't continue without it.

"That's a good girl, rub that clit for me. Is it nice and sensitive? Because it sure sounds like it is. You sound like you are nice and wet too. Just like I like you. Are you? Are you wet?"

"Yes, Sir."

"Good. I can smell you, too. I love the way you smell."

I can't respond; your words are like a fire inside me. I just keep rubbing my clit, moaning out the pleasure, trying to vocalize every last sensation. Your eyes can never see my face contorted with ecstasy or how I look when I ride your cock, but you know each sound I make, and what it means. My thumb strums over and over my clit, and I can hear your breathing getting faster, the chair creaking as you lean forward. I wish you would join me on the bed, but I know it isn't time yet. Everything is done on your schedule during these games. I love surrendering to you. More than you'll ever know. I want to please you.

"Good girl. Now finger yourself while you stroke your clit. I want that pussy ready for me."

I hesitate again, moving against the sheets, trying to find my composure. I can hear the displeasure in your voice when you speak. I hate disappointing you.

"What are you waiting for? I said, 'finger yourself.' You're not disobeying me, are you?"

"No. No, Sir."

"Then why aren't you doing what I ask?"

"Because, I'm afraid I'll come, Sir."

You walk over to the bed. I watch you as you move through our domain just as easily as anyone with sight would. You lean down close to me, wrapping your fingers in my hair, pulling me roughly toward you. I look at you as I cry out, knowing that even without sight, you see me better than anyone else ever has. Because you know what I want. I whimper under your touch, the pain tempered by your soft kiss on my neck and then my lips. But the tenderness in you that I love so much is soon gone as you bite my bottom lip.

"You won't come, because I haven't told you to come yet. You know very well you need my permission before you can come. Isn't that right, darling?"

I swallow the lump in my throat, every inch of me on fire.

Then I speak the words that you love to hear almost as much as I love to say.

"Yes, Sir. That is right."

"And why is that, my dear?"

"Because I belong to you, Sir."

"Good. Now, get those fingers in that pussy."

You use your hand to guide my own fingers inside me. As my cunt tightens around my thrusting digits, my gasp goes right into your ear. You lean in farther, rasping your teeth over my already abused nipple. The flicks of your tongue are timed perfectly with my plunging fingers. I struggle for control of the orgasm growing within me, my breathing punctuated with mutters and groans. You lean in closer, your lips touching my ear as I pleasure myself. For you.

"You really do make the most beautiful sounds. The way your voice cracks when you get excited. It sounds like a barely contained cry. It makes my cock so fucking hard. And when I pull your hair or spank that sweet ass of yours, it sends me almost to the edge. Maybe after you make yourself come, I'll turn you over and spank that naughty, disobedient little bottom. Would you like that?"

"Yes, Sir, I would."

My fingers are moving inside me even faster, the pressure of my thumb on my clit becoming unbearable. Your mouth once again closes over one of my nipples, drawing it between your teeth. I arch under you, my body straining to hold on as I wait for you to give me the permission I so desire. The permission to come. I draw my fingers out of my pussy slowly, trying to calm myself down, but it's no use. As I plunge them back inside me, I know the edge is dangerously close. Even though I know I shouldn't, I beg.

"Please, Sir. Please let me come."

You pull back from me, just long enough to run your hand through my hair and pull roughly.

"Do you really think you deserve it?"

"Yes, Sir. Yes."

My fingers keep moving inside me, until your hand settles over mine. Pushing me aside, your thick fingers enter me, a calloused thumb rubbing my clit just the right way. I expect more rough talk, but instead I get your sweet voice in my ear.

"Come, my darling. I want to hear you come."

That's all I need to hear. All I've ever needed.

BATHROOM
PLAY

Catherine Paulssen

Tienna rushed into the bathroom where Nessa was painting her nails berry red.

"Sorry, hon," she said. "I need to take a quick shower before meeting my mom." She pulled a face and stepped out of her sweatpants. "You don't mind, do you?"

Instead of answering, Nessa watched her girlfriend strip off her ankle socks, shirt, bra and, finally, her red polka-dot panties. A soft sheen of sweat still shimmered on her olive-toned skin.

Tienna shook her head of tight curls and winked. "Like the color," she said with a nod to Nessa's toes.

Nessa grinned and closed the bottle of polish. "Like your ass."

Tienna threw a short glance at the mirror. "Hmm," she said, a bit too casually, shrugging at the same time that she slapped her butt. She turned to Nessa, a huge grin on her face, and blew her girlfriend a kiss. "Thanks!"

While Nessa waited for the polish to dry, she watched as

Tienna's hourglass figure went blurry behind the steamy glass of the shower door. Her arms reached up to lather her hair. She turned around, and Nessa could make out the dark delta of her well-trimmed bush. Tienna flashed a smile at her, a bright shimmer through the haze. The contours of her body became clearer as she took a step toward the misty glass. She pressed her upper body against it, and amidst the drops of water running down, Nessa could see her dark, round nipples and the small pit of her belly button. Her fingertip appeared against the glass and with squeaky moves, drew I LOVE YOU into the steam.

Nessa laughed. She wiggled her toes and carefully tested the polish.

Tienna squealed when she opened the door to the shower. "Hey, what—"

But Nessa didn't let her finish. She grabbed her butt with both hands and pulled her close. "I love you too."

Tienna bit her bottom lip. She slipped the bathrobe off of Nessa's shoulders and pressed her soaped-up body against her lover's, melting into a long kiss.

Nessa stepped into the shower and shuddered slightly as their bodies rubbed against each other. Tienna thrilled her like no other woman she had ever been with, and two years of living together had not changed a thing.

Her hands roamed Tienna's body before grabbing her thigh and pulling her up and closer. Tienna's foam-speckled bush tickled her hip, and Nessa's fingers found their way between her legs.

Tienna moaned softly. "You know my mom is never late," she breathed into Nessa's ear.

"You shouldn't have teased me like that then." Nessa grinned and parted Tienna's pussy lips. "You know I can't resist you and your tiny nipples." She took one between her fingers and rolled it lightly.

Tienna closed her eyes and threw her head back. "Heaven knows I could use relaxation," she sighed. "I got a feeling Mom wants to discuss my job again." She rubbed her leg against Nessa's waist and moaned as she teased her clit until it was swollen and throbbing.

Nessa softly bit her earlobe. "Turn around, baby."

Tienna's eyes were dark with excitement as she pressed a kiss on her nose and then turned in her arms.

Nessa's fingers followed the curves of her girlfriend's body, pausing at her butt to paint little circles. She placed small kisses down her spine, reached for the shower gel and let it trickle onto Tienna's back so that she could massage it into her skin. She spread the foam all over her back and shoulders, cupping her breasts from behind and lathering them with soap. Her thumbs moved languidly over her hardened nipples. Tienna rested her head against Nessa's shoulder and surrendered her body.

"I love how your tits press into my back, baby," she whispered, and Nessa felt herself getting turned on. A surge of heat shot to her clit as she watched little drops of water drip off the tips of Tienna's breasts.

Nuzzling at Tienna's neck, Nessa stared as a stream of foam ran down over her nipple; she grazed it with her fingernails and let them wander farther down Tienna's body until her hands met between her lover's thighs.

"Spread your legs for me," she whispered, unfolding her hand and rubbing Tienna with increased pressure. The hot water poured over their bodies; the soap on their skin made squishing noises.

"We've got to be quick," Tienna groaned, her breathing labored against Nessa's cheek.

"Hmm..." Nessa squeezed Tienna's clit between her fingers. Tienna made a small chortling noise as the water ran into her open mouth. "I don't want it quickly," she continued, ever the tease. "I want to slowly..." She rolled her fingers over Tienna's pussy lips. "...Slowly make you melt."

Tienna gasped and nodded.

Nessa sucked at her flesh, licked at the water running down her skin. "Unless maybe..."

"Unless...?"

Nessa grazed her teeth over Tienna's nipple. "No," she mumbled. "I changed my mind. You're just too hot to be let off the hook soon."

Tienna groaned. "You're so nasty."

Nessa enclosed the nipple and sucked on it. "Not really the best way to make me do as you please," she said with a sweet grin.

Tienna cupped her face in both hands and kissed her. "Make me come. Now," she said. "Please?"

With another kiss, Nessa loosened their embrace. She reached for a small massage toy in the shower's soap rack, turned it on and ran the buzzing head along Tienna's body. She circled it around her bellybutton and directed it farther down, her fingers following the wake of its vibrations rippling across Tienna's skin. Tienna gasped and leaned her head against Nessa's shoulder. She sighed contentedly as the toy began to hum against her clit.

Nessa let the oval head rotate around Tienna's most sensitive spots, but made sure the vibrations only tickled her.

"Harder, baby," Tienna said, nudging impatiently against the toy.

"Louder," Nessa shot back, unfazed by her pleading.

Tienna moaned and buckled her hips. "I want it fast," she whispered beseechingly into Nessa's ear. "I *need* it fast."

"Say it again."

"Damn it, Nessa!" Tienna pushed her against the shower wall. "Stop being such a fucking tease..." She licked at Nessa's lips and grinned. "Get me off already."

Moaning against her lover's lips, she whimpered as Nessa increased the massager's force and pressed it tighter against her clit. She swayed her waist to the rhythm of the vibrations the buzzing toy sent through her hips. She clung to Nessa's shoulders and uttered short, ragged moans. Nessa increased the toy's speed and waited for Tienna to erupt.

And she came, squirming against Nessa, stumbling as the waves of orgasm hit her.

Before she could lose her balance, Nessa caught her in her arms and held her until she calmed down. She stroked her shivering body and savored the feeling of the hot water that engulfed them.

"That was awesome," Tienna eventually whispered into Nessa's ear.

Nessa smirked. "Relaxed enough now to face your mom?"

Tienna laughed. She fluttered a kiss onto Nessa's lips then slipped out of the shower and into a towel.

"I'll pay you back tonight," she grinned. "For the tease as well," she added with a twinkle in her eyes.

HOMECOMING

Jenna Bright

Staring at the hard-hewn planes of the face in front of me, I searched for hints of the boy I'd known, so many years ago. The boy who'd given me my first kiss, late at night in the winter cold, on my parents' front porch. The boy who'd taken my virginity in the afternoon sun on the riverbank that last summer.

The boy I'd thought I would be with forever, until university, and distance, and life pulled us apart.

Except now life had pushed us back together, and I couldn't help but remember the feel of his lips on my skin and his hands on my body.

"You look…" I tensed, waiting to hear which way he'd go. Would he lie and say I hadn't changed in ten years? Or would he finish with "different," his tone suggesting, "worse"?

Neither as it turned out. "God, Sally, you're more beautiful than I could have dreamed."

His words surprised a laugh from me, and suddenly we were

standing there laughing as if we'd never left, never quarreled, never said good-bye.

"Let's go for a walk," I suggested, and he took my arm with a smile.

Perhaps it was inevitable that we would end up down by the river; it had always been our spot, long before that hot, sticky afternoon he trailed his hands up my thighs, tugging down my knickers and replacing them with kisses.

Now, the air was cooler, less heavy with heat and need. But the pulse of my blood, the wanting in my body, was louder than ever.

Ten years, it kept screaming. *Ten years too long.* If I only got one more chance with this man... But that wasn't what we were here for. We were old friends, catching up. That was all.

"And so I knew it was time to come back home," John said, finishing up a story I hadn't even been listening to. I looked up to apologize, caught his eye...and lost my breath.

There. There in his gaze, in the way his looks lingered on my neck, on my skin...I could see heat. Want. I blinked, wondering if it was just a reflection of my own need. But no...still there.

"God, Sally. I missed you so damn much. I missed us."

"Me too," I breathed, knowing exactly what he meant. It wasn't just the companionship, or the love, or the way we made each other feel when we were together. From the first moment I'd felt his hands holding my hips, felt his cock sliding inside me, I'd known. This was something special. Something rare. I had not been with many men since, but enough to confirm what I already knew in my heart. John and I...sex wasn't just physical gratification. It wasn't even just making love. It was something more.

Tugging me down to the grass of the riverbank, John settled me between his legs and pulled me back to rest against his chest.

"Maybe you'll pay a little bit more attention to this story," he said. I started my apology, but he just rested his hands on my thighs and said, "Shh. I never told you why I brought you here, the first time we made love, did I?"

Well he was right about one thing; that was a story I wanted to hear. "No. I just assumed, with us both still living with our parents, it was the only way to get some privacy."

He shook his head, his lips against my hair. "I could have come up with something. No, I brought you here because it was open. Public." A shiver ran through me at his words.

John leaned forward, his breath warm in my ear. "Because there was a chance we might get caught. And I knew you'd get off on that."

Wetness trickled between my legs, matched by a throbbing there that wanted so much, so badly and right now. "How did you know? I didn't even. Not then. Not until years later."

He kissed my neck, and I tilted my head to give him better access. I wanted those lips all over me. I wanted them running up the length of my throat, wanted them hard against my lips, wanted them closing over my nipples...."

"It was your parents' porch that gave it away," he said. "Whenever I used to kiss you good night there, you'd keep your eyes open as we kissed, staring out into the darkness. Took me a while, but eventually I realized you weren't worried that someone would see us. You were hoping they would. So I started taking things further. Grabbing your ass while we kissed, slipping your strap down over your shoulder. And you only ever kissed me harder."

"I never realized..." But now that I thought about it, there'd always been that tingle, even then. That spark inside just thinking of someone seeing how wanton I could be.

John's palms lay flat against the hot skin of my thighs, and his mouth brushed against my neck, driving me crazy. I might not have seen the man in ten years, but I needed him inside me again. Now.

"So, you still like to show off for a possible audience?" he asked, amusement in his voice. I hummed my agreement as his tongue ran along my collarbone. "Good. Because there's a guy in the woods across the river. Watching us."

Arousal jolted through my body. I peered across the water, trying not to be too obvious, but desperate to know for sure. There—a flash of a red jacket behind a tree. John was right.

"You want to show me off, then?" I asked.

John slid the straps of my sundress down my arms, exposing my braless breasts, and my nipples hardened painfully. "Hell, yes."

Careful not to block our watcher's view of my body, he ran his hands up my sides to my breasts, trailing his fingers around my nipples before pinching them tight. My head fell back as I groaned with pleasure. I couldn't see our uninvited guest any longer, but just knowing he was there was enough for me.

"Let's really give the guy a show," John said, placing my hands on my breasts. As I started to twist and pull at my own nipples, his hands returned to my thighs, tracing circles higher and higher until he could pull my knickers aside, exposing my pussy to the warm summer air.

"What do you think he's doing over there?" John murmured. "Do you think he's touching himself? Getting off while watching you? God, I hope so."

So did I. The long, thick hardness pressing against my lower back told me that John was just as turned on by this as I was. No wonder we were such a perfect fit.

John circled my clit, making the muscles in my stomach pull tight, before plunging a couple of fingers straight into me. My hips jerked up to meet him, wanting more, wanting to be filled.

But John's hand wasn't going to cut it.

"Hang on," he said, knowing instinctively what I needed. "Let me lie down."

I heard the fly of his jeans open, then the rustling of the condom packet. Glancing behind me, I watched him roll it onto his straining cock, just as thick and full as I remembered.

"Ready?" he asked.

I nodded.

Gripping my hips, he lifted me up, my knees pressing into the grass on either side of his hips. From this position I couldn't see him, only experience exquisite pleasure as the head of his cock parted my folds and pressed inside me. Slowly, I lowered myself onto him, delighting in every inch of me being filled, the pressure just where I needed it. As I sank down as far as I could, John moaned, and the sound of it made me clench tight around him. I started to move, my hips flying back and forth as I built us both up. John's grip tightened, his fingers digging into me, and I knew he was close.

This was what I had missed. This was why I had never been able to move on, never been able to find a guy who made me feel the way John did. We just worked together. And now we were displaying that perfect synchronicity to the world around us. And anyone who wanted to watch.

I slammed down hard, crying out as every muscle in my body contracted, fireworks going off under my skin. Beneath me, John roared his own completion as he held me tightly to him. I stayed atop him, the muscles of my pussy milking him for every last drop. And as I pushed my damp hair away from my forehead, I saw another flash of red in the woods across the river.

I hoped our new friend had enjoyed the show. Maybe he would come back again tomorrow.

I knew we would.

SIMMERING
DOWN

Kathleen Tudor

W endy dumped her purse on the table just inside the front
door and kicked her shoes off hard enough to send them
flying into the wall. She muttered as she tossed her keys into the
bowl by the door and shucked her coat like it offended her.

Her husband stuck his head around the corner, an eyebrow
raised. "Bad day?"

"Don't even ask!" She didn't normally have much of a
temper, but she'd had to fire two groomers, and her business
had been painfully backed up all day, with customers unusually
vocal about their irritation with the waits. Not to mention the
schnauzer who'd gotten loose and nearly started anarchy in the
salon, and the mix-up of two Pomeranians.

Josh pulled his head back out of view, and Wendy closed
her eyes and let herself lean against the wall, concentrating on
taking slow, deep breaths. She knew better than to push away
the one person who would love, listen to and help her no matter
what, but this had possibly been the worst day of her life and

she was still trying to remember how to breathe.

When she opened her eyes again, Josh was coming down the hall toward her. He opened his arms and gave her a sweet smile, and Wendy collapsed into him with a sigh, letting her troubles go for the moment. She could worry about calling in favors and interviewing new groomers and pacifying angry dog owners later. One good thing about being the business owner: she'd already delegated the massive physical cleanup from the awful day.

"Come on," Josh said. She followed as he pulled her down the hall and into their room. The bathroom door was shut and he went to it, releasing a billow of steam as he opened the door. He pulled her inside and Wendy gaped. The man had apparently located the box of various candles she stored in the closet, and he'd lit them all. The bathroom glowed in the mellow light, and the tub was full of hot water—the source of the steam that floated and swirled in the hot air.

Josh stood behind her as she took the room in, breathless. His hands found her waist and brushed against her body, up to the sides of her breasts, then down to her hips. When they rose again, he lifted the hem of her shirt with them, pulling it up and away. He unlatched her bra and dropped it next to the shirt, then kissed her shoulder as he reached around to unfasten her pants.

Wendy closed her eyes and let herself be swept away by the sweetness of the sensations and the joy of being taken care of. Josh petted and adored her as he stripped her naked, then his own clothes rustled as he continued to kiss and stroke her, pausing only long enough to peel each of his own layers away.

She moved willingly when he took hold of her and gently guided her into the tub. It was a surprise when he stepped in with her, but as they sat together she relaxed into his embrace and let the heat drain some of her tension away.

"This feels wonderful," she said, releasing a deep sigh.

Josh kissed the side of her neck as he brushed her hair forward over her opposite shoulder. "I'm glad." He sat back, and the sweet roughness of their sea sponge replaced his fingers on her skin as he washed her back in slow, massaging circles. Then he pulled her against him and the sponge moved over her shoulders and across her breasts, down her belly and between her legs.

Wendy moaned as he scrubbed her pussy gently with the sponge. She gasped and spread her legs wide when he pressed harder, delivering an erotic sting. She'd felt humiliated the first time he caught her masturbating with the rough sponge, but he'd put her fears at ease, taking surprising delight in the way his wife was aroused by that small discomfort alongside her pleasure.

He took full advantage now, scraping the rough sponge across her sensitive flesh and making her blood heat from far more than the hot water. Then he eased up, teasing the sponge back up along her belly, scraping the roughness against her erect nipples with one hand, and following it up with teasing pinches and caresses with the other.

Wendy pressed back against him, her whole body tingling with the strength of her arousal. The steam filled her lungs, perfumed with the mildly floral scent of her body wash, and she couldn't quite catch her breath. Josh chuckled in her ear, and Wendy shuddered at the vibrations, the back of her neck prickling. His cock pressed hard against her ass, throbbing with his pulse, but he made no demands of her, simply playing her body like a fine instrument, his hands—and that wicked sponge—his tools.

This time it was his bare fingers that dropped past her stomach to that sweet spot between her legs, and Wendy arched back into him, hard, as his fingers teased over her clit. Her breath came faster and harder in the heavy air as he stroked down between her pussy lips and then back up again, his fingers finding that perfect rhythm on her clit as he used the sponge to gently abrade her nipples with his other hand.

Josh kissed her neck and Wendy threw back her head, resting it on his shoulder as he teased her body into boneless desire. He kissed the column of her neck and everywhere else he could reach, his lips soft and his teeth nipping gently at her flesh. She squirmed and moaned as pleasure built up like water behind a dam. Her bad day was not entirely forgotten, but he had pushed it away and buried it beneath the joy and pleasure of the moment. Wendy was more than happy to brush it off and make the day vanish beneath the bubbles on the water, where Josh's fingers were busy working...

She reached beneath the water and grabbed his legs, her fingers digging in as if to anchor her against his efforts to send her spinning into orbit. But he knew her every weakness and he had a full bag of tricks after so long together. Even as Wendy fought to prolong her moment on the glorious edge of pleasure, Josh pinched her clit, hard.

The sharp spike of pain inside the froth of pleasure was like the bite of a cinnamon candy, sweet and hot and too delicious to deny, even through the mild wash of pain. Ecstasy burst within her as his clever fingers eroded the dams she'd erected, and water sloshed over the edges of the tub as the sensations jolted through her and her body responded. Her scream echoed in the small confines of the bathroom, and she bit it off, moaning and mewling in pleasure instead as Josh chuckled and stroked her.

She went completely limp against him as his hands went from teasing and inflaming to calming and petting. He stroked her face and kissed her cheek, and she turned to kiss him on the mouth. Their tongues teased and enticed, sweetly rather than passionately, as they connected.

"Now," Josh said, kissing her nose and pulling away, "if you lean forward I can wash your hair and you can tell me about your day from hell."

Wendy smiled and leaned forward. "Somehow everything seems a little more manageable, now."

NAILED

Giselle Renarde

Mandy never used to hold my hand in the car. This was new, this one hand on the wheel, one pressed into my palm thing. I loved the innocent romance of it. Handholding was Betty and Veronica, complete with the love triangle. Ours was an all-female version, equally contentious, and focused entirely around big, beautiful Mandy.

Pink polish. Her fingernails were glossy, but they shimmered purple in the blue light from the dashboard. Every time we hit a bump in the road, they dug into the meat of my hand. It hurt so good.

But if I thought my kitten had claws in the car, that was nothing compared to the bedroom. Her daggers really came out when we got to my place. I brought out my thickest strap-on dildo and she dug those treacherous nails into my ass so hard I screamed.

She knew just how I liked my pain.

"God, that hurts." I wrapped my legs around hers and held

her in my arms. "Feels incredible. But it hurts."

"Thought so."

"I love it, Mandy." I growled like a bear, bucked like a bull, until my dildo couldn't take the heat and popped right out of her pussy.

I slowed my thrusts, guiding that slippery shaft back inside her unfathomable wetness. After that, I fucked Mandy gently enough to stay inside. Cocks had minds of their own. Even fake ones.

She writhed beneath me, pushing her big tits against mine so our nipples played and pressed together. When we kissed, she dug her nails into my flesh and squeezed. My body leapt, and I gasped like pain was my oxygen.

"Too much?" she asked, teasing, knowing very well it wasn't.

"No, baby, feels good." I hugged her body tight, forcing my fake cock up inside her. The strap stroked my clit with every thrust, but there was a part of me that wished I could feel her pussy muscles clamping down on my dildo. If only there were artificial nerve endings I could hook up to feel that pressure.

Mandy's fingernails closed the sensation gap, and she must have known it.

"More," I pleaded. "Make it sore."

I wanted to feel the hurt all week. I wanted to feel it on the days she spent with Aisha instead of me. When I was alone in bed, wondering if Mandy was alone too—but too afraid to call and find out—I wanted to feel the sting of my girl's fingernails, a reminder that she loved me too. The pain would serve as a memento of our lust.

But Mandy teased me, tracing her nails up my back so lightly it tickled, making me shiver as I shoved my cock in her.

"Harder," I begged.

"I don't want to hurt you," she said, always teasing, taunting, dancing her fingernails across my skin.

"I *want* you to hurt me." I thrust in her, making her whimper and cringe and tighten the muscles in her thighs.

She hesitated, tracing her fingers down my ass, gently, too gently.

"It's not like anyone's going to see the marks," I said—a loaded statement, and she knew it. I could tell by the look in her eyes.

Exclusivity.

I had tried not to push it too hard, but she knew I wanted exactly what I offered. I wanted her to be mine and mine alone, just like I was hers. Exclusively. There was no other girl I wanted. Just Mandy. Why couldn't she be satisfied with just me?

The smile on Mandy's face did it. I bubbled from the inside out, kissing her cheeks, her nose, her lips as I rocked inside her. She dug her nails into my ass and I arched away from her mouth. Gasping, I cobra-posed on top of her full body and cried out, "Oh my god!"

It hurt like hell, but I loved it. She was right about me. She was totally right.

"Sometimes I look at you," I said, "and my insides just feel like they're gonna come bubbling out."

She rolled her eyes like she didn't believe me, so I fucked her harder, sliding one hand around her front. Slipping it between our sweat-soaked bodies, I found her clit. Her eyelids fluttered closed as she arched back, and the sight of her like that, so close to ecstasy, made me want to stop everything and take a picture.

Then Mandy scratched ten red lines into my ass, and the sheer sting of it moved my hips in double time.

"I look at you, Mandy..." I grunted as I fucked her. "I look at you and my temperature rises. And then you touch me and I'm so hot I can't stand it."

She squinted, squealed, threw herself at my strap-on. "When you get hot, I get hot."

"Yeah?" I asked, grinding against the hardness, getting myself off on the strap while she writhed beneath me.

"Oh yeah, baby. Big time."

Mandy dug those lacquered nails into my fleshy ass. My body heaved itself against hers. My hips went crazy against her. I knew I could get myself off like this today. I was just about there. We could come together. We could do it.

"How hot are you now?" she asked, panting, her voice thin as linen.

"So fucking hot!"

Her razor nails dipped down the small of my back, slicing a path to my shoulders. The pain egged me on, like a brand, a mark of permanency, a tattoo. I fucked her so hard she screamed, finding my ass once again and driving her nails into my flesh.

"You really like this, don't you?" She was laughing and panting at once.

There were no words to express how much I loved her nails. I loved the sharp stabs and lingering sizzle, so I kissed her, melting and melding into her mouth.

She tore me to shreds as we came together. The flood and gush of our orgasm took everything from me. All the energy I'd had was suddenly gone, and my thighs ached. We were drenched in sweat, panting, straining, drained.

I pulled out of her, letting my cock rest on her thigh as I lay on my side. Staring. God, she was beautiful with her hair stuck to her temples, soaking wet. She was so beautiful I could die.

My back shrieked with pain and I could just imagine how it would feel when I took a shower—the soap, the sting, the hot needling water. For some reason, that made me think about Aisha, and my mood swung down into hell.

Mandy must have read my face, because she sighed. I thought I knew what she'd say: "Don't start," or maybe, "Just be happy we're together right now."

But I was wrong.

She said, "You know I love you."

"I know. I love you too." I kissed her chest, her shoulders, eager to show her just how much. I sucked her breasts and for a moment she was quiet.

Then she said, "Aisha. I love her too."

I pulled away from Mandy's nipple and nodded. My lip quivered, and I bit it until my mouth filled with the metallic sting of blood.

"But she's so jealous now," Mandy went on. "She never used to be. In the beginning she was mature about our situation, just like you are."

Usually, I didn't like hearing about Aisha, but hope welled in my heart. Did Mandy mean... Was it over between them?

"I had to walk away," she said, and I felt the weight of her heartbreak in my chest. "Jealousy is relationship poison, and once it's in your veins that's the beginning of the end."

For the first time, I really understood how much Mandy loved both Aisha and me. I had secretly painted our open relationship with a much blacker brush than it deserved. All this time, Mandy was full of love for us, but Aisha and I were too competitive to see each other's worth.

My back and my butt stung from Mandy's nails, but I couldn't enjoy the sensation just yet. Now that I had exactly what I *thought* I wanted, I realized I wanted more.

"You've got so much to give," I told Mandy. "And you know what? So do I."

She looked at me and smiled like she knew just what I was going to say next.

"Let's talk to Aisha." I'd usually feel embarrassed to suggest it, but the marks Mandy left on my skin had opened me up to new possibilities. "Let's do more than talk."

"That's what you want?" Mandy asked, leaning up on her elbows.

I nodded. "If she wants it, I want it too. We could be good together, all three of us."

Mandy leaned in to kiss me softly, and then she whispered, "Aisha's got nails like the devil. You're going to love her, babe."

PERK OF
THE JOB

Cheyenne Blue

Is that Ralph in doggie daycare?"

Mohinder, my boss, leaned carelessly against the door of the examination room, his white coat hanging from one finger. I took a minute to compose myself before I answered.

"It's Ralph."

"What's wrong with him this time?" Mohinder ran a hand through his shaggy black hair.

I longed to smooth it for him. Actually, there was a lot I longed to smooth on my boss's rangy body.

"He's fine. It's his monthly check."

In truth, I knew that Ralph, my rescue puppy, was bounding with health. But Mohinder had suggested monthly checks and I wasn't going to argue. A perk of the job as a veterinary nurse was free care for our own animals.

"He'll bankrupt us. How about I double your salary but rescind the free care for Ralph?"

Old joke, but I pretended to consider. "No go. It would break

Ralph's heart if he couldn't see you."

Ralph adored Mohinder, but he'd survive. Me, on the other hand…

The day passed quickly. I worked with Mohinder, and with the grumpy senior partner. I was equally efficient with both, but I didn't find the need to rest my hand on the senior partner's forearm to emphasize a point, didn't flirt with him over the dressings tray. With him I was strictly professional.

It was no hardship to work alongside Mohinder, hoping for the not-so-accidental brush of bodies as we passed between the examination table and the bench. I loved listening to his low voice crooning to a recalcitrant animal, his gentle hands soothing their fur. The thought of those long fingers on my body had given me any number of spiraling flights of fancy.

Staff pets were left until last. It was a long day. Surgery with complications. A feral cat that escaped and ran amok. So when Mohinder called for me to bring Ralph in, everyone else had already left for the day.

Ralph pattered in, grinning as only a Staffy can. Mohinder bent to pat him and Ralph went into ecstasies, rolling over to display his huge stomach to be rubbed. Between us, we hoisted him onto the examination table.

"He's a credit to you, Mel. This isn't the same malnourished dog of six months ago." Mohinder's voice was warm, and I smiled with delight.

Mohinder was close, only a finger's breadth away from me. His white coat brushed my bare arm, and I fought to suppress the shiver

"I'll give him a vitamin shot, but I think he's doing well."

I turned away to draw up the shot, and when I swung back Mohinder was scratching Ralph behind his ears, crooning to him in low tones. My breath left my body in a shaky exhalation.

If only Mohinder would talk to me with the same warmth. If only his hands would soothe my body instead of Ralph's.

Our fingers fumbled as I handed him the syringe and it fell to the floor, protective cap still in place.

Simultaneously, we both crouched to retrieve it, and our fingers touched again. The heat in his skin made me pause. He stilled as well and I fancied I felt a connection leaping and skittering between us like a wild thing. I didn't remove my hand. I was acutely aware of my heartbeat, pounding furiously, the sprinkling of dark hairs on the back of his hand, and his warm, spicy smell. As the seconds stretched and he didn't remove his hand, I dared to look at his face. He was staring at me, and there a twisted look of naked longing I couldn't mistake.

Mohinder wanted me.

Before I could talk myself out of it, I leaned forward and kissed him. For a fractured second, his lips hesitated under mine, as if he wasn't sure the moment had arrived or how he should respond. Then he grasped my shoulder and pulled me to him, taking my mouth with a sweet ferocity.

I kissed him back, welcoming his tongue into my mouth, grasping his shaggy hair, pulling him into the kiss.

He groaned—in passion or because his knees were aching from our crouched position I wasn't sure—but then we rose to our feet, and the distance between us was gone, and we were wrapped in each other's arms.

Desire, long suppressed, ignited and swept through me, instantly wild and out of control. I pushed aside his white coat, burrowed under his shirt until I could touch skin: warm, soft, a scattering of hair on his belly.

Mohinder slanted his mouth firmly across mine, and his hands tugged at my uniform shirt until the buttons gave way and he could push it off my shoulders. Then his mouth was on my breast, suckling a nipple to a hard point through my lacy bra. I shucked the shirt away, and wound my fingers into his hair again,

A tiny part of me screamed that this was not one of my better ideas—I still had to work alongside him after this. Workplace affairs were a terrible idea and falling in love with your boss was an even worse one. But I pushed that thought firmly out of my mind. Mohinder dropped to his knees and his mouth pressed to my belly. I leaned against the examination table for support as his lips bumped their way lower, sending jolts of pleasure across my skin.

I bumped against something behind me. Ralph! How could I have forgotten him? But my dog was asleep, nose on his paws. I shifted so that I wouldn't disturb him and Ralph was forgotten as Mohinder pulled down my panties and dropped even lower, burying his face into my pussy. His nose nudged my mound and his tongue pushed its way through my folds, finding and circling my clit.

Ralph could have rolled off the table at that moment and I wouldn't have cared. Mohinder's tongue stroked in a steady rhythm sending circles of pleasure spiraling outward through my body. I gripped the table and stared through unfocused eyes at the top of his dark head. My boss. On his knees in front of me. Maybe not loving me, but certainly wanting me. As I wanted him.

The heady thought was enough to push me over the edge, and I came, gulping air convulsively, my body jerking in huge spasms, every muscle taut.

Mohinder rose to his feet. His face was flushed, his hair damp.

"Mel—" he began.

I kissed him again to shut him up. Whatever he was going to

say, now wasn't the time. We'd come this far—I'd be damned if we would stop now.

It was my turn to explore his body, and I went straight for goal. I unzipped him and slid my fingers inside his pants. His cock twitched underneath my fingers, warm and hard, oh so very hard. I dragged him through the gap in his clothing.

"Careful," he said, in a strained voice.

I'd thought I was being too rough, but when my fingers circled his tip, it was wet with precome. I slid my fingers along his length—not too long, but wide and solid. And hard. Then he took control, pushing me against the table, raising one leg so that I was open and exposed to him. He moved between my thighs and his cock bumped on my inner thigh, followed by a blunt press as he found his goal. One solid, forceful thrust and he was inside me.

His hands found my hips, and he started to move. I looked down along our bodies, to where we joined: curls of wiry black against my own clipped soft brown. I closed my eyes to better absorb the sensations, but when his movements got faster, harder, I opened them again, wanting to watch him climax. He was watching me too, all glittering eyes and warm brown strength.

He held me hard, setting the pace. Each thrust, each swelling movement of his cock brought me closer to an edge I thought had passed, at least for this time.

As I built inexorably to a second climax, a thought wound through my head: *We are good together.* And then I was coming hard, clenching around him, and he was coming too, his face contorted, his eyes still locked with mine.

As we came down to earth, our bodies still locked together, his hand caressed my cheek in a lingering touch.

"Mel," he said, "my beautiful Mel. I've wanted to do that for so long."

I took a leap of faith. "Me too. I've wanted you since the first week I worked here."

He smiled. "Only wanted me? I've loved you at least that long."

It seems free pet care wasn't the only perk of the job.

A.M. WOOD

Rosalía Zizzo

Returning from the restroom and passing by the cold hearth, axe propped aside it, I slide into bed next to my warm husband and curl into the space at his belly that hugs my backside perfectly. *Spoons*, I think. *Mmm...* As I roll to the side, I notice his erection saying good morning to me while he sleeps, so I stop and look down at him, mentally processing my options. I could return to my position beside my warm lover, but my thoughts would never allow me to sleep.

Hesitating briefly, I slowly draw nearer because I don't want to wake him. I look from his peaceful face to his cock and back again before creeping forward. He'd appreciate the surprise, wouldn't he? Advancing, I gaze at his penis while crouching close to his skin where the heated memory of his shower the day before drifts to my nostrils. *Irish Spring*, I think. *Smells so manly. My man.* As I approach his erection and blow lightly on the head, it twitches gratefully in response. It encourages me to lift the sheet from his legs and open my mouth to glide my lips and tongue over his upright member, which hardens and swells even further.

Oh, Doctor Anthony Michael Wood. You really are the love of my life. Remembering when we met in school, I ruminate on all of our struggles to get where we are now, to get the diplomas and credentials, to achieve those goals that were really no surprise to anyone but us. We were so shy. It's amazing we met at all at that college mixer, both of us timid and uncomfortable but obviously looking for something (or someone) different. When he showed up at my door the next day with a bouquet of roses, I knew my life was about to change forever. I just didn't know at the time I was going to marry the sweetest, most generous lover I have ever known. And a lover who would melt into the hottest, most wicked man I have ever had in my bed.

I wrap my lips around his cock and suck, swirling my tongue around the ridge around the head's base that's like the brim of a hat. While sucking, I lick the velvety length as I enjoy the soft and warm skin clothing the stiff rod. I place the tip of my tongue on the opening, and, tasting the salty fluid, I close my mouth around him and suck more vigorously. He mumbles something unintelligible after he stretches and kicks away the remaining covers, and I aggressively devour him until I feel my own arousal build and I hear him moan.

When he starts rapidly thrusting into my mouth, I know he's awakened. I remove my lips from around him and lift my head to meet his eyes and whisper with a smile, "Good morning." He promptly cups the back of my head with his hands and pushes me toward the soft thatch of dark hair at his groin, returning me to his dick where I nibble along the length before continuing to suck the swollen crown.

"Morning," he groans sleepily.

Increasing my speed, and feeling my own increasing need, I

pet his thighs and continue to devour him while he bucks into my mouth, tickling my face with his pubic hair and lifting his hips from the bed. He raises his body again and again as I suck him farther into my throat, and he pants with increasing fury.

"Mmm," he moans. Reaching down to tangle his fingers in my hair, he sounds his pleasure with each of my licks along the shaft and every frantic squeeze of his thighs. We earnestly paw at each other until his breathing sounds laborious, and he grabs my hands to still my sucking and drag me into his warm, naked arms.

"Come here, my naughty nurse." Gazing at me hungrily, he swats me on the backside playfully before kissing me on the neck and rolling me over onto my back.

Spreading my legs with his knees, he opens my pussy lips with his thumbs and gently begins to massage around my opening and over my clit. When my clit starts to swell, he wets his middle finger with his tongue and ever so lightly moves slow circles around the growing bead before stroking along the inner walls of my engorged lips. As I relax into the languid move-ment, brush the back of my hand across my mouth and start to moan, he clutches my hand as he has done many times before and presses it to his lips, kissing the wedding band as well as the fingers surrounding it before kissing a trail up my arm and then turning his attention back to my clit and lightly stroking it until I can't help but alter my position and order, "Lie down."

After uncontrollably flipping over to be on top of him, I spread my legs and set my knees on either side of his hips. As I struggle to position myself, he spanks me again. "Here. Let me give you a hand," he says.

"Ha ha."

"You're a beautiful, bad girl," he tells me before wrapping me in his arms, and I giggle when I feel him strike my ass for the third time. "Oh, I want my wife so badly." He squeezes my shoulders and runs his palms over my body, paying particular attention to my ass and thighs. "Let me give you what you deserve."

I know exactly what he means.

Feeling his chest against my own, I slowly sink onto his hard erection, which fills me completely and causes me to mumble into the hair that remains stuck to the side of my face.

"Yeah," I moan.

With each subtle movement of my hips I hiss into his skin, before I raise my head to ride him rapidly and then collapse back onto his furry chest where I hear his heart thud against the side of my face as he hugs me to him. His cock feels so thick. I feel myself stretching around him as I ride, my orgasm starting its steady climb with each constant upward thrust of his hips, while he employs a finger on my clit, continuing to stroke it, gradually increasing his tempo. The tingling spreads throughout my body like a gust of wind sprinkling fairy dust onto my shoulders and hair.

An image appears in my mind of my very own doctor donning a white lab coat, his icy stethoscope wrapped around his neck. The image excites me and reminds me that we have traversed many snowcapped mountains and lived through many mornings to get here, but it has all been worth it. The axe leans against the wall near an empty fireplace, but our lovemaking has made it seem as if we were near a roaring fire.

He hugs me to his chest as my heat builds, and I squeeze my doctor's body between my thighs, subtly riding him. Every beat of our hearts, every rise and fall, brings us closer to our destination. Like a sunrise about to break, the sensation increasingly glows orange and pink. I squeeze around him tightly, frantically, reaching the point of no return.

When I sense his initial spurt by the jerk of his cock, I instantly erupt—like the sun's rays bursting as it rises over a hill. Releasing the air from my lungs, I tense and rock through each rippling wave after wave, while he flips his eyes skyward and gradually slows his bucking until he thrusts once or twice more and then drops his head to the pillow with a sigh.

Making love sure beats chopping wood to ease the morning chill that permeates our little abode, and now our bodies emanate their own warmth. Twisting to swing an axe so it drops heavily onto a dry log takes effort but perhaps not as much effort as a gentle romp brought on by early morning cock worship, and definitely not as much effort as twenty years of marriage. Our fireplace sits empty, but our heat warms the bed as our breathing levels, and I curl into the crook of his arm.

STEAL
THE KEY

Amy Glances

S hould I steal his room key? I don't want to run the risk of knocking and him not answering. Plus, if I steal the key I can sneak in and surprise him. Take him against his will—well, not really against his will, but against his pretenses.

The problem is we're both in long-term relationships, his longer than mine. I'm technically on a break and he—I don't give a fuck what he's on, I just want him in me.

How did we get here? We worked together a couple of years ago. It was purely professional, and then I couldn't resist sending him an inappropriate email.

"Let's get out of here."

He responded, "Where are we going?"

And I wrote, "I'll take you anywhere you want to go."

It was on. It was fun and exciting and dangerous. We were risking our jobs, trusting, though we barely knew each other, but having one hell of a good time.

I always pushed it further, and he always topped me. That's

what I liked about him.

I sent him a message. "Do you have room on your desk for my elbows?"

He wrote back, "I have to go to a meeting. Let me wipe the sweat off my brow and collect my thoughts."

He came back from his meeting, and responded to my question. "No, we'll have to tie your elbows behind you."

I thought I'd found my soul mate. I wrote, "I was just testing your boundaries."

"You can't see them from where you're standing," he wrote back.

My panties were wet, my palms were sweaty, and I wasn't getting an ounce of work done, but I didn't give a damn.

This went on for weeks. I knew it was risky, professionally and emotionally, but I couldn't stop. We told each other all the intimate details of our love lives, and the sordid, sick details of the love lives we wanted to have: lust, punishment, pleasure, fear. In short, we wanted to use each other's bodies for everything we had dreamed of, but couldn't talk anyone else into doing. Whatever we wanted, it was okay because it was all a fantasy. I told him I wanted him to hold me down or up against a wall and force himself onto me. He told me he wanted to tie me up on a chair and watch a couple of hot prostitutes eat me out.

The rule was always the same. We could email, wink and even whisper if no one was in earshot, but we could never act. We could never be alone together, because we both knew what would happen.

I'd invite him to lunch. He'd decline. I'd try to talk him into going out for a drink, but he'd never accept. He said we could never be alone together. But then one day I broke the rules.

I told him I was going over to his office to talk to him after work. He said maybe some other time. I waited ten minutes and went anyway. He was still there, and he never stayed late. He had a surprised smile when I walked in.

In his office I tried to keep my distance from him. He said he was curious about my motivation for flirting with him. I told most of the truth, "I thought it would be a confidence booster and make the day go quicker." I didn't tell him that I wanted more.

No one else was in the building, so I felt safe. He wanted me to look at something on his computer screen, so I leaned over him. I knew there was no turning back. I put my hand on his thigh and slid it over his cock and rubbed hard.

"We can't," he said, just as he always said.

I put my other hand over his mouth. His dick was hard under my hand, so I pushed him to the ground. He pushed me off of him and said he should go home.

I unzipped his pants, and he shut his office door. He ripped my blouse open and embraced me. He held me close for a moment, and then he said he wanted to, but he couldn't. The turmoil was written all over his sad eyes and furled brow. Then he kissed me. But it wasn't a right-before-we-fuck kiss. It was a this-may-be-the-last-time-we-ever-get-to kiss. It was long and hard and slow and passionate, and I began to tear up. He could feel my wet tears against his cheeks, and he held me closer. He whispered his apology in my ear, even though it had been me who broke the rules. Then he zipped his pants and he left.

I knew I had to move. I looked for new jobs in other cities. I found one. And then I moved nine hundred miles away.

That was two years ago.

We kept in touch with an occasional email, a little flirty once in a while, but nothing like the messages we used to send.

Then one day he sends me a message saying he's coming into

town and wants to go out to dinner. I give him my number, he calls me, and we make plans to meet at a restaurant.

I try to dress sexy-sophisticated. I don't want to look like an easy mark, even though I am one. We meet at a seafood restaurant downtown. He's there when I get there. We say hello and hug. He's nervous. I'm excited.

We talk about work and family and friends over dinner. We keep it light. I try not to look into his eyes for too long, because I know he'll see the longing in them. We laugh a lot and have a great time, just like I knew we would if we ever got the chance. He invites me to his hotel room across the street for a nightcap.

We walk over, close but not touching. We get to his room and have a few drinks. He's still nervous; he's not being forward and he never comes close to me. He's sitting on the bed and I'm on the chair and we're still laughing and the sexual tension is so thick you can see it in the air, like a cloud. I can tell he's thinking about it; he keeps glancing at my legs and clenching his jaw. My pussy is soaking just thinking about it, but I dodn't want a repeat of what happened last time, and I can't wait another two years. We talk and drink for an hour or so, and then I tell him I better go. He looks disappointed, but says he's glad we had a chance to catch up.

I notice his room key is lying on the nightstand close to where I'm sitting. Should I steal it? He might resist a little less after I've left and he's resenting himself for not making a move.

I stick it in my pocket when he's not looking. I'll wait until he's asleep, and then I'll wake him up with a sexy surprise.

He walks me to the door and offers to walk me to my car, but I tell him I can make it. He gives me a long hug, and I can tell he doesn't want to let me go.

I walk back to the restaurant and have a few drinks at the bar.

I'll give him time to jerk off and fall asleep. Also, I'm working up *my* courage.

Finally, it's time. I walk back over to the hotel and go to his room. My heart is pounding in my chest. I slip the room key into the door and ease it open.

Just like I hoped, he's in bed. I slip out of my clothes and into his bed next to him. He begins to sit up, but I push him down and kiss him hard. He's wearing a T-shirt and boxers. I pull up his shirt and rub his muscular chest.

He wraps his arms around me and kisses me back. I reach under his boxers and he's already hard. I have to have him inside me.

I'm soaking, and I know he's thick and throbbing for me. I swing one of my legs over him and force his cock into me. He moans. I come all over him. I only have to slide up and down his now-slippery dick a couple of times before he pushes me off of him and turns me over. I arch my back awaiting his thrust.

Instead I feel the slippery wetness of his tongue. He licks around the outside of my cunt lips then works it inside my hungry pussy, searching and probing every inch. I'm in heaven. His tongue moves slowly but confidently. I'm turned on picturing his face between my legs. I crane my neck trying to see his tongue entering me. My pussy starts gushing. I can't see it, but I know his face must be soaking. He lunges his tongue deep inside me and I scream. He does it again and again, and I begin to fear that I'm going to have an orgasm that will shut me down and I won't be able to fuck him. Just as I'm about to go over that edge, he pulls his tongue out and slides over me.

He thrusts into me slowly. I'm starting to climb that hill of ecstasy I know I won't return from, but I don't care. He moves his cock in and out of me, leans forward and licks my nipples softly and then kisses me, and I don't care if I live or die after this. I whimper. His steady thrusting keeps me in the throes of my orgasm. I grab his back with all of my life and I can feel his cock bulging, almost ready to release. I open my eyes. He locks his eyes with mine and explodes into me, my nails digging into his back and his arms squeezing me tightly. I cry. He holds me. We giggle and pant.

We are holding each other, recovering from our orgasms and enjoying the way our bodies feel. After a long quiet moment, he breaks the silence.

"I saw you take the key."

ONE HOT
WET NIGHT

Veronica Wilde

The sweltering Mississippi night breathed down Erin's thin camisole as she watered her azaleas. She wiped the back of her neck, hoping her hair didn't tumble out of its knot and make her even hotter. It was almost ten o'clock, but the steamy July temperatures stayed high long after moonrise. Still, she lingered outside, fussing over her flowers. The house might have air-conditioned comfort but it also had her husband, Matt, watching TV on the couch.

Ex-husband, rather. It had been five weeks since they'd formally agreed to divorce, and it would be three more weeks before she moved into her new apartment up in the city. Right now they were coexisting in a tense civil arrangement, Matt sleeping in the spare bedroom. They didn't argue, but they didn't talk either, and Erin found that watering the front-yard flowers at night was a welcome escape.

She wiped her damp forehead. Three more weeks until her new life started. She'd be single again at thirty-six, living in the city—and dating. Were any sexy guys her age still single? Would they be interested in her, or would they all chase college girls? She glanced around her quiet neighborhood. Everyone on her suburban block was married. Not that she would want to date any of her neighbors anyhow—the only good-looking guy was Peter across the street and he was married to a beautiful realtor named Jessica.

She moved on to pulling up a few weeds. Her long hair was starting to come out of its knot and her thin white top was sticking to her damp skin. But she didn't want to go inside yet.

The crack of a hammer echoed through the quiet night. She turned to see her cute neighbor Peter erecting a FOR SALE sign in his lawn.

She headed across the street, surprised. "Since when are you and Jessica selling?" she called.

Peter straightened. He was shirtless, his brown hair tousled. She swallowed at the sight of his tanned torso.

"Since our lawyers decided that would be the fairest way to proceed." He tested the sign's sturdiness and glanced at her. "I thought everyone knew. We're splitting up."

"I'm sorry to hear that." She hoped the words sounded more sincere than she felt. "Matt and I are splitsville too—but he's keeping the house. I'm moving to a place in the city."

Peter's dark eyes studied her. "What happened?"

She shrugged. "Just life. I mean, he cheated on me last year but I kept thinking that it would be too hard to start over. We finally both agreed it was time to move on."

"Sounds like me and Jessica," Peter said. "I knew we weren't in love anymore, but the idea of leaving her and starting over just seemed like so much work."

"But you're gorgeous," Erin blurted. "How could you ever have trouble finding someone?"

Her face went hot with embarrassment in the streetlight. What had possessed her to say that? She wiped away another bead of sweat from her forehead, hoping he would blame the heat.

Peter gazed at her, a knowing smile spreading across his face. "You know what I'm going to miss about this house?" he said. "The pool."

Erin hadn't gone skinny-dipping since college. But she tried not to show her nervousness as Peter led her around to the pool deck. The dancing light of the pool washed over his face and chest as he calmly unzipped his jeans and kicked them off. Maybe, she thought, he would swim in those black boxer-briefs he was wearing.

Nope. Peter kicked off his underwear and strolled down the deck, apparently unembarrassed by his erection. Good god, he was fit. His sculpted chest and hard stomach were met by narrow hips and long legs. She hadn't seen another naked man in the flesh since her wedding thirteen years ago. And though she'd often fantasized about Peter when she was alone with her vibrator, the glorious masculine reality of his body was far more impressive than her imagination.

He dove cleanly into the water and surfaced, his dark hair plastered to his cheekbones. "I'm waiting."

Erin swallowed. This was something else she hadn't done in over thirteen years: strip naked for a new man. She pulled off her damp white tank and then, fingers shaking, unhooked her pale pink bra. As her breasts came into view, her face filled with heat. Oh god, standing here topless in her shorts was more excruciating than being fully naked. Quickly she slipped out of her shorts and panties and before he could get a good look at her pussy, she dove into the pool.

Whew. The cool water felt like heaven on her overheated skin. She took a deep breath of relief as she surfaced.

Peter treaded water close to her, his dark eyes locked on her face. The greenish reflection of the underwater lights gave his handsome face a sexy, devilish look. "I bet your husband is going to miss that beautiful body of yours."

She laughed nervously. What could she say? *And Jessica must be crazy to let a gorgeous man like you get away.* "Hopefully someone else will appreciate it."

He pulled her against his chest, his skin warm even underwater, and kissed her. His lips moved on hers like a spell, melting her body with an intoxicating excitement. Peter was kissing her, sexy Peter from across the street was kissing her and holding her naked in his arms, his hard dick prodding her body. She swallowed as he pulled her into the shallow end and ran his fingertips between her legs.

She opened her thighs for him, two of his fingers slipping into her pussy. This wasn't something her husband had been good at, but Peter rubbed and stroked her pussy with consummate skill, driving her desire into something wild and thrilling. She clung to him, burying her face in his neck and moaning as he fingered her.

Without warning, he lifted her out of the pool and laid her on the edge. A moment later his tongue was dancing over her sensitive sex, circling her clit until she moaned, then probing inside her. She pinched her nipples, whimpering helplessly. She couldn't believe her hot neighbor was really eating her out here by his pool. But she needed more.

"Fuck me," she whispered. "Please, Peter."

He grinned. "Hold on."

He hopped out and disappeared into the house, returning within moments with a condom. She felt dizzy with anticipation as he led her to a poolside lounge chair and opened her legs. So many nights she had fantasized about fucking other men, about feeling a new cock thrusting inside her. Now as Peter's hardness drove inside her sensitive slit, a primitive groan escaped her. His cock felt so good, driving deep and fucking her fast, an unstoppable rhythm of pure masculine desire.

He rolled her onto her stomach and reentered her, taking her from behind. Cupping her breasts in his hands, he worked his hips against her, driving her excitement higher. A whirling storm of wet, blissful pressure was swelling inside her and as Peter played with her nipples, her orgasm broke in searing, rhythmic throbs that seemed to roll through her entire body. Peter bit her lightly, a long groan escaping him as he came.

"Goddamn, you are sexy," he sighed. "You know how many times I've fantasized about doing that?"

She slipped back into the pool, the water cooling her orgasmic flush. "Really?"

"Hell yeah. Every time I used to see you getting the mail..." His grin widened. "You know, you're the first woman I've dated since Jessica. If this counts as a date. I've been married so long, I don't know the rules anymore."

"Me neither," she admitted.

Peter kissed her, a light brush of a kiss that inflamed her again. "Well, maybe we can practice the dating thing on each other."

"Deal." She kissed him and hopped out, gathering her clothes. "But right now I should probably get home."

They kissed good night after she dressed, and she slipped back out into the street. Her hair was dripping and smelling of chlorine, and her makeup was washed off; Matt would know she'd been skinny-dipping. But that was his problem, she thought. She was starting a new life that was none of his business. When she walked into the house, she saw he was asleep on the couch. Smiling, she headed to her bedroom. Her new life was off to a great start—and she already had a date.

THE DISTRACTION

Louise Hooker

A melia ran one hand nervously through her red hair while she held the other one to her mouth and gnawed at her fingernails. Her eyes were focused with a hawk-like gaze on the cordless handset that stood—silently—in front of her. It was just within arm's reach, and it would only take her a moment to dial the number she had committed to memory. She reached for it once, twice, drawing back at the last second. She finally freed one hand to rest on the table next to the phone. Immediately, she began to drum her fingers along the polished wooden surface.

The doctor had said that he would call back today. Amelia was sure of that. She knew she had asked him how long the results would take. She glanced up, over the distance of her living room, to the small clock that hung to the right of the entertainment center. It was only one o'clock in the afternoon. So everyone would be returning from lunch. Maybe her test had not been the first to be run this morning, she reasoned with herself. After all, Doctor Somer was a well-respected fertility specialist. He had *hundreds* of patients. Plenty of other couples going through the same troubles conceiving, like Darren and her. This thought did nothing to comfort her as she drummed her fingers harder.

She barely registered the sound of the front door opening, and the familiar echo of her husband's footsteps through the foyer.

"Hey, honey," Darren said.

Amelia gave a little start and whirled around. She clasped both her hands tightly behind her back. Darren sighed, shaking his head as he tossed his keys onto the nearest table. There was a hint of sympathy in his deep-blue eyes as he narrowed them at his wife.

"I take it the doctor hasn't called yet?"

Amelia shook her head, unwilling to trust her voice. After all, what if the doctor had bad news? What if it was her? What if her eggs or uterus were no good or unstable or *something* that would keep the couple from realizing their dream of parenthood? She could not deal with that. She wanted to be a mother. She wanted to experience giving birth to her children. What would she do if that phone rang and took all her dreams away?

"Honey?" Darren asked gently.

She snapped out of her thoughts. Slowly, her eyes fell to the small, wrapped package in Darren's hand. He grinned as he noticed this, nodding to the red-and-white-heart-patterned package. Running a free hand through his blond hair, he shrugged.

"Happy anniversary, Amelia. I got us something."

Amelia blinked. In her preoccupied mental state, she had completely forgotten that it was their third wedding anniversary. She unclasped her hands and pressed them to her lips.

"Oh my god... Darren, I'm *so* sorry. It's just, with this stupid fertility doctor thing, I completely—"

But Darren held up his hand, and nodded toward the staircase.

"I said I got *us* something. But we have to open it in the bedroom, okay?"

"What? Why?" Amelia asked, but she was already making her way toward the stairs.

Darren followed behind her, gently laying a hand on the small of her back as they cleared the flight of stairs. He steered her into their room, positioning her in front of their bed. Amelia frowned as she looked down at the crumpled bedding. In her haste to await the doctor's call, she had not even made the bed that morning—something she *never* forgot to do. Dishes, laundry, those things were some of the chores Amelia easily pushed aside. But she liked a clean, pressed bed. She shook her head and turned, surprised to see that her husband stood less than an arm's length from her. He had her trapped between him and the bed.

"Darren, what—wait. How are you even home? It's only one," she asked.

He grinned, reaching around her to set the package down on the bed.

"I took the rest of the day off. Now open the gift."

He had an impish grin on his face, and it was a little infectious. Amelia was fairly certain that I'm-up-to-no-good look was one of the reasons she had married him. She turned, laughing as Darren made no effort to move, and ripped open the package. The paper revealed a plain, cardboard shipping box about the size of a standard jewelry box. She ripped through the packing tape to reveal his gift.

"What?" she asked, pulling the item out.

They were handcuffs. But not just any handcuffs. They were made of leather—she could tell just by the smell. There was just something inherently masculine in the smell of the material. They were black, connected by a silver chain. The fasteners of the cuffs were also silver and looked something like overlarge buttons.

"Third anniversary is leather," Darren whispered.

He took the cuffs from her, opening one and clasping it around her right wrist. Amelia felt a fluttering in her stomach that she had not felt in some time. She shook her head, a nervous laugh slipping past her lips.

"Darren...what is this?" she asked.

"I thought you might want to try something new."

He pushed her back onto the bed, and she gave a surprised yelp, followed by a laugh. With some assistance from Amelia, Darren moved her up toward the head of their bed. He strung the loose cuff behind one of the bars of their headboard, pulling her left wrist up to be clasped by it.

"Pull on them. Test them out," Darren said.

Amelia did as asked, finding that she was very trapped. She grinned up at her husband.

"You forgot to take off my clothes, you know."

Darren grinned, all but tearing off his shirt. "So?"

Amelia felt a hot blush color her face, and a bright smile spread over her lips. Three years of marriage, and two years of dating before that, and he could still make her blush. She nibbled at her bottom lip, reducing her smile to grin.

"We've never done this before," she murmured.

Darren was bent now, kissing and biting at the nape of her neck. It sent a pleasant tingle up and down her body, causing her to squirm against her restraints. He moved his lips lower, moving down the V-cut of her blue blouse. He flicked his tongue within her cleavage, causing Amelia to squeal.

He pulled back, smiling down at his wife as she struggled against the cuffs. She groaned, trying to pull her legs out from underneath him. But he had all of his weight on her now, and she was not going anywhere. He grinned at her a bit longer, causing her to groan up at him.

"What's wrong?" he teased.

He knew very well what had Amelia so bothered. She loved undressing her husband, feeling his hardness break free as she undid the button and zipper on his pants (and she could tell now that he was more than ready to be freed). But her restraints kept him far out of reach. She could feel the heat growing in her nether regions as Darren finally freed himself. He slid his hands slowly up her legs, underneath her black skirt, and grasped at her panties. With one tug, he yanked them down.

He was over her again, kissing her roughly and kneading her breasts through her top. She groaned as she felt her wetness begin to roll down her thigh. He chuckled softly as she pulled as hard as she could against the leather cuffs.

"I need you," she moaned, squirming even more.

He did not respond. Instead, he lowered his hand and ran his thumb over her clit. Amelia cried out, and Darren was careful to keep the pressure on as he positioned his cock at her entrance. With no warning, he thrust inside her, keeping his thumb in place as he moved in her.

Somewhere downstairs, Amelia was vaguely aware of the phone ringing, but in the heat of pleasure, it felt more like a distant memory.

"Yes, baby, please!" she cried as her husband pumped harder inside of her.

Darren thrust faster, and it was not long before Amelia felt the heat build up until she could take it no more. With a single, strangled cry, she felt herself come, her pussy tightening to squeeze around Darren. Moments later, Darren echoed her cry, coming inside of her.

He collapsed beside her, huffing and puffing as he reached up to undo the cuffs. Amelia rubbed her wrists and smiled, kissing him lightly on the forehead.

"Happy anniversary," she laughed.

He laughed, followed by, "Hey, did the phone ring?"

Amelia nodded. "Yeah."

He arched a brow at her. "But...it could have been the doctor."

She shrugged. "It won't kill him to leave a voice mail."

CONNECTING
FLIGHT

Salome Wilde

The status for the flight from Detroit to Pittsburgh read NOW
BOARDING. Kit clenched her fists, forcing herself from
indecision into action. Grabbing her carry-on, she headed for
the restroom. Once inside, she went straight to the mirror...to
remember another restroom, another mirror, and Lauren.

"Looks good," said the stranger, smile wide as she stood
behind Kit in the hotel bathroom. "Very good."

She was tall and strong featured, with a short, spiky haircut,
small round glasses, and an androgynous look that Kit was
surprised to find attractive. A conference name tag like her own
hung around the woman's neck. Kit tried to read the reversed
reflection.

"Hi," the stranger said, a flirtatious flash in her hazel eyes.
She brushed against Kit's arm as she stepped forward to wash
her hands.

Kit blushed and, without need, washed her own. She'd never
been picked up by a woman before and never expected to be,

especially not in a public bathroom.

She eyed Kit's name tag. "So, you're the lovely Kit Haffkin from the University of Kentucky." She extended a wet hand. "I'm Lauren Woods, from down the road at Michigan State."

Kit hesitated then took her hand. "Um...nice to meet you." She couldn't remember the last time she'd felt so awkward.

"Dreadful keynote, eh?" said Lauren casually, lightening the mood but not releasing Kit's hand. "Had to escape."

Kit nodded but didn't pull away. "Me too."

"In the mood for further insubordination?" Lauren's expression was lit with mischief. She squeezed Kit's hand and, when Kit smiled, leaned in to kiss her.

Kit's shock was devoured by a warm, arousing embrace. Lauren's lips claimed hers as her free hand circled Kit's waist. Just as a thread of guilt was seeping in about Jeff, the kiss ended and a dazed Kit blinked up into a hungry gaze.

Lauren licked her lips. "Wow."

Kit's mouth tingled. "Yeah," she breathed.

"C'mon," Lauren said. "Let's be truly unprofessional."

Kit nodded, feeling nervous and wildly excited.

"This way to rebellion in room three-twenty-five." Lauren grinned as she tugged Kit out the door.

Kit's pulse raced as they scrambled down the hallway. She heard the audience respectfully applaud from the distant conference room. Hand in hand at the elevator, Kit's bravery grew. When the doors opened, Kit did the tugging.

Smoky mirrors reflecting her impulsiveness, Kit pressed the button for the third floor then pressed Lauren to a wall. The kiss was more intense than the first, heightened by Lauren's throaty moans and the dream-like atmosphere. *I'm making out in an elevator*, Kit told herself as she wrapped her arms around the unfamiliar waist and wide hips, *with a woman I just met*. She shivered as Lauren pressed a thick thigh between her legs. Kit yelped and clung as the elevator dinged and the doors opened onto an empty hallway.

The fantasy deepened as Lauren reached the door to her room and put her hands over her head and spread her legs. "Time to play body search for the key card." Kit hastily looked around; not even the cleaning staff was in evidence. Lauren wiggled her ass impatiently, and Kit patted her down firmly until she found the desired object in a pants pocket. Lauren took the card, swiped the lock and pulled them both into her room and onto her bed so fast Kit could only gasp and giggle.

Kit fed on drugging kisses, rich with Lauren's soft and demanding tongue. Tenderly bold fingers soon unbuttoned her blouse and removed her bra. Her breasts were cupped and squeezed, nipples licked and sucked with a reverence that felt not like fetishism but recognition. And when Lauren removed her own shirt and the tank beneath it, Kit eagerly offered worship of her own. The experience was beautiful, delectably new.

Lauren needed little encouragement to slip out of her khakis and show off her ample body. "I may not have much," she announced as she flung away her boy-cut panties, "but at least I have a big ass." As they both laughed, Lauren began to remove Kit's slacks and panties.

Kit tensed.

"Relax," Lauren said. "You'll love it."

"But I haven't..."

"I know," Lauren replied with her irresistible smile. "The time is right for a first time." She kissed Kit softly and whispered, "And I'm the one."

What Lauren said wasn't boasting; it was true. Kit's curiosity had met Lauren's assertiveness and a powerful attraction had bloomed with breathtaking speed. And Kit's doubts easily yielded to Lauren's confidence. Skillful fingers toyed with the softness of her labia, tugged gently on her curling pubic hair, dipped into moistness. When Lauren slipped a finger inside, Kit moaned.

"Please," she whispered, and Lauren bent to feast.

It was so good, so sweet. And when Lauren shifted pace, thrusting two fingers in and out while sucking her clit and teasing it with the tip of her tongue, Kit came so hard it made her scream.

Climactic shudders gave way to a shower of tiny aftershocks, and Lauren's rosy, wet face popped up from between her thighs. "Damn, woman, you know how to come."

Kit smiled, panting, but stopped herself from admitting she'd never come so fast in her life. Lauren climbed up and kissed Kit deeply, and Kit tried not to flinch at the strong taste of herself. When their lips parted, Lauren laughed. "Trust me, it's ambrosia."

Kit rolled her eyes and deflected embarrassment by asking, "My turn?" She wasn't sure she was ready or able to give the kind of pleasure she'd just received, but she could try.

Lauren chuckled. "Easy there, little tiger." She kissed Kit's nose and pushed her back. "You just enjoy the afterglow." She hopped out of bed, pausing to pat Kit's rear. Then she headed for the bathroom. "Gotta pee!"

Kit's heart was hammering as the door clicked shut. She rose and dressed quickly, legs wobbly. She knew she wanted more. Not just more sex, but more Lauren. But she couldn't. Lauren's innocent comment had brought her back to reality and she had to stay there. "Little tiger" was Jeff's nickname for her. And she'd betrayed him. She felt like crying as she rushed out the door and fled down the stairs to her second-floor room. Jeff deserved a partner who didn't cheat on him and Lauren deserved honesty. She'd failed them both.

For the rest of the conference, Kit vacillated from fantasies of spending the weekend in bed with Lauren to guilty calls to Jeff. She admitted nothing and felt too much. A perusal of the conference program told her Lauren was presenting her paper the next morning, and she spent the day in bed, watching HBO and feeling lousy. When it came time to present her own on the last day, her head swam with self-pity and guilt as she scanned the audience, both hoping and fearing Lauren would be there. She wasn't.

Only when she was checking out of the hotel did her mood shift. The clerk presented a note left for her, and she tore it open immediately.

> *Dear Kit,*
>
> *Funny how someone can be so pushy then let something she wants badly slip through her fingers, isn't it? Don't know what spooked you enough to run off like that, but it must have been something big. I didn't want to chase you, so I just made myself scarce for the rest of the weekend.*
>
> *If I came on too strong and freaked you out, I'm sorry. It's just who I am. I won't contact you again, but I'm putting my business card in with this note in case you get back to Detroit sometime. If you do, look me up. I'll be waiting.*
>
> *Lauren*

Kit read the note over and over on the plane back to Kentucky. And she kept it hidden at the back of her sock drawer at home, even long after she ended the relationship with Jeff for what he called "no good reason." She finally retrieved it nearly a year later. Waiting for the cab to take her to the airport, she had stuffed it into her purse.

Only now, standing in the Detroit airport restroom, just before noon, staring at herself in the mirror and purposefully missing her flight, she took out the note and her cell phone, then dialed.

"Lauren Woods."

Kit swallowed. "Lauren, it's Kit."

"Kit?" She paused. "Wow."

"I'm at the Detroit airport." Her heart hammered. "Missed my connecting flight."

Lauren was silent.

Kit rushed on, trying to keep her voice light. "I was thinking about spending an insubordinate weekend at a certain Detroit hotel."

"Were you, now?" Lauren replied, a smile in her voice.

Kit closed her eyes, remembering that smile. "With a woman I fell for at first sight but let slip through my fingers."

"Second chances don't come often," Lauren said.

"No, they don't," answered Kit.

"See you there," came the quiet, confident reply.

And we'll get it right this time, thought Kit.

WILD NAKED BANDITS FLEE THE SQUARE CONSPIRACY

Nikki Magennis

He wore skintight leggings that should have been illegal, a polka-dot kerchief, and a moustache that curled at the corners. Wayward hair. Killer cheekbones. He was lurking at the punch bowl, staring deep into the lurid orange sangria as though it were poison. I couldn't resist.

"What have you come as?"

"It's just the way I'm standing," he said, and took a swig from a bottle of gold tequila with his pinkie stuck out.

"That doesn't work," I said, frowning. He swooshed tequila around in his mouth. His eyes slinked over my costume—black bodysuit with a tail and squint eyeliner whiskers—and the curves under it.

"Kitty. Do you know," he said, leaning suddenly right up against me and whispering in the fake pointy ear stuck on the side of my head, "who these people are? Do you know what they *do*?"

"Uh, I came with Johnny. He works in the museum, anthropology, I—"

"Ssssss!" He gripped my arm and tugged me into the hall. Actually, he whisked me, and for some reason I let myself be whisked, through a doorway and into a room which stank of fried chicken and cigar smoke. Overcoats and fake-fur jackets were heaped on the bed. He closed the door.

"You mean," he said, voice loaded, "*The Commandant.*"

"Excuse me?"

Now Zorro clutched me like a desperado, his face a whisker away. He licked his lips, and I smelled licorice. He searched my eyes and, boy, I'd never known a man to look at me so nakedly.

"Well, that's fresh," he said. "You really don't know."

"Huh?"

"He can say peace in seven languages, Kitty."

"So he has a gift for—hey!"

Suddenly, he was diving at the bed and pushing coats onto the floor.

"We don't have much time," he said, "Call me Gabriel. Do exactly as I say."

"What in hell *are* you doing?" I said. "I'm not getting in bed with you."

"A lady with morals!" "Gabriel" stripped the sheets off with a flourish. "Give me a hand, would you?"

I opened my mouth but no sound came out.

"Behind you, the sword."

A crescent scimitar hung on the wall, some kind of ceremonial thing, I guess. I hesitated, wondering at the wisdom of handing some nut in spandex an offensive weapon.

"Kitty," he said urgently, "I hate to break it to you, sugar, but your date is the head of an international arms-smuggling syndicate! You're in great danger!" he cried.

Now, a girl like me knows enough not to use dialogue tags

in contemporary fiction, but this guy really did cry out. And whether it was the pinot or the way he acted like a boy scout on ecstasy, I found myself swept up in the excitement.

"Do you really want to disappear and spend the rest of your life bound in sexual servitude to a criminal mastermind?" Gabe asked.

"Well now, if you put it like that..."

"*Kitty!*"

I smirked and handed him the scimitar by the rope-bound handle.

He slashed the sheet and twisted it into strands, tied them end-to-end and fixed the shabby looking rope to the brass bedstead. There was a film of sweat on his brow and his turquoise eyes practically glowed.

I watched as he zipped to the open window, balls jiggling in his lycra trousers.

(What? They were hard to miss.)

Anyway, he scrambled over the sill and his pert buttocks tipped up and waved in the air. I guess I got a little dizzy. He swung round, tested the knot and signaled frantically.

"On the count of three."

Five minutes later I was hanging from our homemade rope with friction burns on my palms and this guy's face scrunched up against my crotch.

"Mmm," he muttered. I agreed.

We slid, rather than climbed, to the ground. Gabe didn't hang around.

"Take cover!"

He raced toward the inky shadows of the park across the street, and leapfrogged the iron railings in one jump. I took a moment longer to walk to the end of the fence and enter through the open gate, but we met on the other side without any problems. I couldn't see much in the dark among the looming vegetation and witchy-shaped trees, but I could smell that hot, spicy tequila smell and just kind of—I don't know, feel him somehow. Like you sense a puppy is about to jump on you.

"Come on!"

And he was off, running toward the duck pond. Behind us, the windows of the flat beamed with light. Someone put on "Disco Inferno." There was a shout. Then a crash.

And then there was a scream.

Maybe somebody spilled punch onto the white shag rug, or maybe my moustachioed freak had a point. I stood for a moment in the wet grass and thought of Gabriel's tight little ass. His earnest chocolate-brown eyes. I turned and followed.

At the pond a streak of white fled by. Even in the gloom he had a finely turned body. Lean but muscular. I couldn't see more than a smudge of his cock, but the shadow of it swinging side to side was enough to make my mouth water.

"Break the trail," he hissed as he waded in. "Strip and follow me."

What the fuck? The kinky kitty bodysuit didn't leave much to strip, and I enjoy breaking municipal bylaws. I chucked the suit in the undergrowth and left my cat ears on for luck.

Goose bumps peppered my skin as the cold water sloshed up to midthigh. Zorro was waiting.

"That's it. Need to wash the scent off you." He started scooping water and splashing me, prompting some choice expletives and a couple of perky nipples that he gallantly ignored.

"There's a safe house nearby," he said, pointing toward the bandstand. It didn't look that safe to me, being open on all sides, but he explained that it gave him the perfect vantage point to see our enemies approach. "Besides," he added as we walked over, "I have protection."

I wondered if that stretched to condoms, because by then his schlong had popped up to join the conversation. We were soaking wet, and my whiskers were smudged, but it seemed the icy pond water had given him a stimulating zing. He stood under the pergola roof of the bandstand with hands on hips and dick pointing proudly toward the heavens.

"Ready to dig in and wait out a siege?" he said. I tried to avoid looking at his dong, but the coy act doesn't really wash with me. And he was peering at me intently. Just as I thought we were about to get intimate, though, he made this terrible groan.

"What is it?"

"Leeches." He pointed at my wet, mud-smeared body.

"We're in King's Park, not the effing Amazon," I said, but not before he'd slapped me on the ass. I batted him away.

"Get off! Not leeches!"

He paused.

"Leaves!" I said, peeling a wet beech leaf from where it had stuck to my stomach.

"Are you sure?" he asked, plucking another dark blur from my breast. "May be best I check you over."

"Go ahead," I said, dropping my voice a couple of gears.

He was thorough as a monkey, running his lithe fingers over me and prodding at every twig and piece of flotsam to check it wasn't attached to me by a set of teeth. When he got to the crevice between my legs, he went very, very carefully, slipping a fingertip between my tender lips.

"Oh!" I said. His hands were cold.

"Kitty," he said, pressing my clit. His moustache twitched in the moonlight.

Then I heard the dogs and everything bristled.

Gabriel didn't miss a beat. He was on me in seconds, knocking me to the ground.

"Why, you don't beat about the bush, do you, Mister?"

"Play along," he whispered, "We need to convince them we're lovers."

He may have been deluded, but I have to admit he was a fine actor. He squirmed and burrowed into me like a condemned man making love for the last time, and kissed me for extra veracity—a wild, passionate kind of kiss with extra tongue. Our eyes locked.

"Oh boy. I'm either nuts or in love."

And voila, we were method acting the part of a couple caught in flagrante delicto. Or perhaps that should be al fresco?

The dogs padded up to the bandstand, panting and smacking their lips. I whimpered a little—just for authenticity. Gabriel obliged with a heroic thrust of the hips that pushed him balls-deep inside.

"Hi-yo, Silver," I whispered, impressed. We may have been on the point of being eviscerated by a couple of rabid Alsatians, but for the moment I was as stuffed as a Kalamata olive and thoroughly enjoying myself. Gabriel bit my shoulder. I started frigging my clit up against his abundantly frizzy pubic hair.

Right on cue, like every dewy-eyed, curvy-assed spy-whore you ever heard of, I started screaming in Swedish.

Any devious assassin would have bet his Glock that I was having a massive Saturday night eye-roller.

"Frances!"

It was Johnny, closely followed by the guy with the orna-mental swords. For the first time, I felt scared.

"Step away from her," Johnny barked. I noticed he'd stopped to put on coat, scarf and leather gloves before he came out to rescue my honor. Behind him our gracious host stood with folded arms.

Inside me, I could feel Gabriel losing his edge.

"Gary, for Chrissake," the sword guy spoke through clenched teeth, "you left your pills behind again, didn't you?"

Though Gabriel's penis was slipping out of me, he still held on tight. I felt his hands on my lower back. They were shaking.

I leaned in and breathed in the scent of pondweed in my lover's hair. He swallowed hard. I saw the mass of trees beyond the bandstand, the path lit silver by the moon. I squeezed Gary's shoulders tenderly. Johnny had been a crap date, anyway, I reasoned.

"Head for the gates. Don't look back. On the count of three," I whispered, "Are you ready, Gabriel? One, two…"

FADED GOODS

Vida Bailey

The little bell jangled as I pushed open the door and walked into the shop.

I didn't remember the place opening, but I was sure I'd passed the faded blue window repeatedly in my morning haze, on the way to the bus stop. It looked dingy, dun-bleached glass bottles in the window, no real effort made at a display. And right beside it, a shiny modern convenience store that bustled. It was a strange attempt at competition. Till now, I never went in. Nor did anyone else, at first. Why would they? It was the kind of shop eccentric old proprietor-ladies in slippers lurked in. Some old dear who scared the children.

She wasn't that old, though. Weirdly, she was starting to collect customers, I noticed, as I passed by on the way home. Young people, women and couples. I caught glimpses of her through the cracked door and then around the town. A dumpy woman, middle-aged and unremarkable, invisible in shirts and jeans and sandals. The circle of chest that showed above her shirt was sun-browned, starting to wrinkle.

Each time I saw her, I was intrigued. She wasn't just unseen because of the liminal status to which so many women her age are relegated. She hugged the wall, dowdy in her ill-fitting clothes. And yet there was something in her that made me look twice. I wondered what her name was.

I heard her laugh ring out from the closed door of the shop as I passed by, joyous, rich and dirty. It seemed fluid and easy, oiled as if from frequent use. I thought about being the one to make her laugh. Would the body beneath the figure-hiding clothes be lined and weather worn as well?

More customers were entering the shop. Was it for the service? Finally taking the plunge, I found myself standing in a tiny room with half-bare shelves.

"What can I help you with?" She stuck her head around the inner door. From behind her, preceded by giggling, two girls with dyed hair and piercings appeared and kissed her goodbye. They paraded out the main shop door in their short skirts and stompy boots and she watched them go, fondly, as if she'd forgotten I was there. I was more bemused than ever, standing in a tiny retro shop-space, staring at faded cereal boxes and smelling the musky perfume of two teenage punkettes and their youth. It couldn't be all about cornflakes.

I gestured to the door she guarded.

"May I?"

She shrugged and smiled. What was *in* there? Potions for young witches? Would I be sacrificed to some blood cult? I swallowed a nervous laugh and stepped past her through the door. My mouth fell open. The room couldn't have been more different from the faded, depressing decor of the front of the shop. Front was the right word. Out there held a despondent small-town shabbiness, unloved and off-putting. Inside was

another world of rich colors and shining shelves laden with...
sex toys. She walked past me and tapped me under the chin.
I closed my jaw with a self-conscious *clop* and tried to stop
gawping. I was surrounded by vibrators and massagers and
nipple clamps. The walls were adorned with all sorts of leather
things for which I had no vocabulary. Everything was shiny
and scary and...*fun*.

"Looking for something specific?" She was watching me
with amusement. I shook my head frantically and tried to find
my voice. "I've been expecting you; you've been working up
the courage to come in. Are you sure there's not something in
particular you want?" Her voice became kind, lost its mischievous edge. Oh god, she thought I was a timid customer and she
was reassuring me.

"Ha, no, really! Honestly, I had no idea. I just knew you
weren't selling cereal and cheap tights, and my curiosity got the
better of me. A sex shop? In Bayville?"

"I do a lot of my business online. The shop-front keeps the
more conservative citizens happy. The truth is, I kind of like it."

I picked up something off the nearest shelf and put it down
again hurriedly when I realized it was a cock ring. The weird-
ness of the moment made me blunter than I meant to be.

"You don't look like a sex shop owner." I had the grace to
blush, but she just smiled.

"What did you expect a sex shop owner would look like?"
There was no good answer to that. "Younger? Sluttier?'" I
worried she was reading my mind.

"Could we have a coffee?" I blurted it out, feeling uncouth.
She frowned.

"Would you be asking me that if I'd sold you a pint of milk
and a Mars Bar?"

"Oh! I really would. Though, no offense, your chocolate

looks like it's been sitting there for a decade." She grinned, appeased.

"Well, it is a few years old, in fairness. No one ever buys it, my front works pretty well. Though I do sometimes attract more senior citizens than I'd like."

"I would love to have a coffee with you."

She raised a skeptical eyebrow.

"Why is that, exactly?"

"You must know a lot of *stuff*," I said in my best Bill and Ted voice, not wanting her to think I'd been stalking her. She laughed. "And I see you round town and you look so... I'd just love to hear your story."

"I knew a lot of stuff once, yeah. Now...well, now I give a lot of good advice." Her voice was soft. I put my head on one side and looked at her. She relented.

"Tomorrow at six?"

I beamed. "My name's Sam. And here's my number." I wrote it down for her and shook her hand. Her grip was warm and firm. I nodded and left without a word.

On Thursday she charmed me. Sadie. Not a date—when I arrived, she was in the middle of inventory. For each product I counted, she listed its virtues and limitations, until I was well-educated and trying to hide a hard on. Her laugh was rough and sweet at the same time, her eyes bright. Her movements were calm, and the conversation flowed surprisingly easily until I asked her how long she'd been single.

"Let's just say it's been a long time since I've practiced what I preach. And that I'm in the right business." She twinkled a distraction, but I hung on to the slippery topic.

"You dress to discourage attention."

"Yeah. I know. Why do you care?"

"You're so confident. Why hide?" She shook her head, half-exasperated, half-nervous. Perhaps she was flattered too?

"It's time to finish up."

I stood with her.

"Can I come upstairs?" She opened her mouth to say no, but she didn't. "You don't have to do anything you don't want to. But it would be sad to miss out on something you do want to do. I'm safe, I promise." It took a beat, but then she reached for my hand.

Her apartment was airy and cozy. Her bed was an old black brass one; the worn and soft duvet had tiny white starflowers scattered over it. It felt like clouds when I sat down. She stood in front of me in her voluminous shirt, fidgeting.

"Oh, Sadie. Stop." I put my hand out to gentle her. "There could be kissing. You could show me your favorite toy." She stepped in to me where I sat on the bed and relaxed against me. Her warmth and closeness, her mouth on mine made me lose my breath. She climbed over me and worked her way under the duvet.

"Lie down with me?"

I wriggled in beside her and she pressed her body up against me. She sighed at the contact as if she'd come home. I held her and whispered,

"Have you been lonely?" She nodded. "What happened?"

"Ah, Sam. Nothing dramatic. Just sometimes life changes and you get left behind."

I kissed her face, her shoulder. I ran my hand over her stomach, ignoring her when she tried to shift it away from the soft flesh there. I bent over and kissed her middle, shaking my head. "You're lovely. It's okay." I held my palm over her pubis, cupping her. I kissed her again, holding her like that. "Will you show me your favorite toy?" She nodded, rolling over toward her side table, trapping my hand between her legs. She took out something smooth and purple, shaped like undulating hills. She pressed a button and it buzzed. She reached out with it and touched it to my nose, so I could feel the vibration. I sniffed, wondering if I would smell her on it.

"*Tsk*. I clean it scrupulously!" I pulled her clothes down, and watched as she slipped the toy into herself, adjusted complicated settings. "Are you piloting a starship with that?" She laughed.

"I kinda am." There was a smile in her voice, but the tension under it showed she was turned on, nerves and vibrations collecting in her. I ran my hands over her chest.

"Can I?" She nodded. Her breasts were small, plump and soft under her shirt. Silver lines traced the sides. Her nipples stood up firm when I stroked her, ran my wrists over them. I touched my rough cheek to the side of the breast nearest me, kissed the stretch marks that patterned it. She groaned and pushed the toy into herself with more force. I sucked her nipple into my mouth and she worked harder, cupping the back of my head with her free hand. I worked my hand under her leg and grabbed the softness of her inner thigh. I heard the vibe climb higher and she pushed hard against me and started to shudder, her nipple rock hard in my mouth. Her hips snapped, and I could hear her heart pounding. I licked and bit the other nipple and her ass lifted off the bed, thrusting. She gasped and called and came, legs shaking. She switched off the motor and I reached for the stilled toy, slipped it out of her and ran it up her middle, touching the slickness to her nipples. I sucked them clean and she writhed at the sensation. I pushed her clothes off completely.

Naked, she looked years younger. I thought she was gorgeous, soft and curved and marked by life. She had strength in her muscles and a worn ease in her own skin she probably didn't value. Her body was worn by time, yes, but still calling.

I put my hand over her cunt and cupped it again, all the

sensation and sensitivity. She closed her legs and rolled toward me. Squeezing her knees up, she held my hand tight between her thighs. I kissed her. Slowly, deeply.

"I'd love to learn how to do that for you. Make you come. Will you teach me? I kissed her again and my fingers pushed inside her wet lips a little. She shifted farther onto my hand, and I was in the heat of her.

"Darling boy, I think you're the one teaching me."

PUZZLE PIECES

Rachel Kramer Bussel

I'm leaning across the dining room table, my elbows precariously placed in one of the few spots where the wood isn't covered by jigsaw puzzle pieces, straining to secure a key piece of the Tropicana in its designated spot. We've been working on the two-thousand-piece Las Vegas Strip puzzle—one I thought we'd finish in a weekend—for a month, so every match is a mini-victory. I've just lined up the edges exactly and am ready to look for my next victim when I feel a slap on my ass that makes me gasp. I don't dare turn around to look at my boyfriend, Roger, but instead pause right where I am, drop my head, close my eyes and wait. His hand comes down again on my right cheek, and I whimper. When the third blow lands, this time on my left cheek, heat is racing through my lower half. I wiggle my ass a little, hoping he will lift up the hem of my dress and pull down my panties.

The next blow is harder than those first few, though with him, they're all pretty hard. I shift, threatening to send precious piles of sorted pieces onto the floor. "You better be careful, Maxine," he says, that sweet, sexy edge of sternness in his normally calm voice; he doesn't need to finish the sentence. That edge makes my nipples harden, and suddenly I long to strip off all my clothes and lie across the table, puzzle be damned, giving him access to any part of me he wants. I don't care that technically the blinds are open and our neighbors, if they squinted, could see in. He nudges my legs wider apart and scrapes his nails up the back of one thigh, along the curve of my cheek, then down the other. The next two blows have me whimpering. I almost put my head down on the table, but I don't. I know how hard he's worked to sort all the pieces for us to pick through; he's methodical like that, whereas I'm drawn to every sparkling billboard or gleaming light.

I'm getting so wet between my legs, and if I were to open my mouth, I'd surely drool. He has that effect on me, even after five years—*especially* now, actually. Sometimes all he has to do is look at me across a room and I completely forget what I'm supposed to be doing. I focus on holding my pose, my elbows digging into the wood. I have no room to spread out, not like in our bed, where I can get up on my hands and knees, or spread my legs as far as they will go. Any sudden movement would threaten all the work we've done, and as much as I'm getting frantic for my spanking, I like what the puzzle symbolizes too much to ruin it.

Roger finally lifts my hem, and somehow him staring at the wet fabric of my sheer black panties is even more mortifying than staying in place. He touches me there, lightly, barely a touch at all, and my insides clench, hoping his fingers will go deeper, but all he does is press the wet fabric up against my pussy. I know he can feel how badly I want him, and I also know that because of that he is going to go at his pace, not mine. I try to cheat and shift my hips just enough to push myself back toward him, but he simply moves his hand away and gives me another smack.

It's getting more and more challenging to stay where I am; I'm balancing on the balls of my feet, my calves stretching, my entire being primed for what will happen next. The best part is that he knows exactly how eager I am, how much I want it, how much I can take. Roger sometimes seems to know me better than I know myself, regarding sex or otherwise. It's a wonderful and sometimes maddening thing, to have to catch up to his insights into my psyche, all the more so when it comes to being spanked. I love that he's aware of exactly how aroused his slaps make me, how each blow sends me further and further into that space where I feel like I could die happily right that very second. I love that his smacks always land right in the perfect spot that makes everything jiggle, that even the harshest blows make me instantly want more, harder, faster, want it never to end.

But because he knows me so well, he knows how to drive me absolutely mad. He knows I hate waiting, so he makes me wait. Sometimes when I beg for him to put something—his fingers, his cock, a toy—inside me, in my mouth, my pussy, my ass, he just laughs and holds me down with one strong hand while he strokes his cock with the other, letting me look but not touch. I'm sure those times must drive him mad too, but either he's better at hiding it or he likes the tease, the wait, the agony and the ecstasy of denying me what I most want. Or maybe it's that he knows if he makes me wait, by the time he lets me open my mouth and spread my legs I'm so eager I barely know what to do with myself.

I'm thinking about the way his cock feels in my mouth while he gives me light taps on my upper thighs, ones that I'd almost prefer he not even bother with. They are so light I know they're just designed to tease me, to see if I'll ask for more or be patient.

Sometimes I manage to hold out, my desire to be a good girl for him outweighing my body's urgent signals to me that it will not be happy until I'm hot all over, until my skin stings with the fresh pain of him pinching or biting or slapping me.

He pulls my panties off, then uses those big hands to hold me all the way open, his fingers pressing my asscheeks wide, his thumbs teasing my labia apart. I drop my head as far as I can without grazing the table, my hair falling in a sticky, sweaty mess around me. I often hold him open just like that, watch as he clenches for me, beckoning me to enter him, but this is different. He's never looked at me so blatantly before, not in the middle of the day, certainly not spread across the dining room table. I wonder what he sees there, what he wants to see. And then I stop wondering as he hoists my hips up and drags his tongue along my wetness. I whimper and feel the tears rush to my eyes. It feels so good, except for the part where I can't move, where I can't plant myself down on the table and fully indulge in the warm maneuverings of his tongue.

I'm not sure how much more I can take, but I'm too proud to ask to move. He's got to know that I'm dying here, that I am so ready for more, that I might have to risk ruining our puzzling in order to get the prize of the full force of him on me. Finally, he pulls me down onto the floor with him. Usually, he prefers our bed, but sometimes neither of us can wait. We don't talk; we don't have to. I love telling him every dirty thought that enters my head, every twisted fantasy, but right now I need my mouth for something else. I push his shorts down, not wasting any time taking them all the way off. Allowing myself only a single glance at how hard and glistening and straining his cock is, I place my mouth around the head. I slowly lick, my tongue circling the swollen ridge, even though what I want is to take it all the way down my throat.

The thing is, we are like that puzzle, in a way. We fit together perfectly, no matter what we're doing. I know how to read each groan he makes as my tongue winds its way along a carefully curated tour of his most sensitive spots. He knows that when he reaches for my back, lets his hand rest on me, it gets me even more excited. Before he can come, I shift around, fling my dress off, then climb on top of him. I guide his cock into my waiting wetness and lean forward, smiling down at him. His hands hold me in place, pressing my hips even as he slams his hips up into me.

We are like our own jigsaw puzzle, the difference being that with us, there are infinite ways we can fit together. I love that we have the rest of our lives to try them all.

VERY, VERY WELL

Kristina Wright

We haven't been together long, Sam and I. It's been not quite a year, which I guess is a long time for some people I know, but it takes me a long time to get to know someone. To feel like we belong together. To want to get experimental outside the bedroom. It's not that I don't have a kinky streak—I do! And I'm open-minded enough to want to try even the things that don't necessarily turn me on, just for the sake of making Sam happy. Because, really, turning *him* on turns *me* on.

I could blame it on a repressive upbringing and the intense fear of being known as a "bad girl," but really I just think I'm a romantic at heart. I want to be in love before I let down too many of my shields. Sex didn't happen until we'd been dating for almost two months. To be fair, our dates had been spread out and sporadic, with one or both of us needing to call it an early night. We had agreed that when we were finally naked together—and it didn't take long to know that it was a when and not an if—we didn't want it to feel rushed. Maybe he was just agreeing with me to be chivalrous—he's definitely that kind of dude—but we waited. And that first time was...earth-shaking. We were holed up for thirty-six hours in his apartment on the twelfth floor and only came up for air to eat and hydrate and use the bathroom. From there, we were inseparable and it wasn't much longer before I realized I was very much in love.

But falling in love with someone doesn't mean you know him, really *know* him—that takes time. And it took us some time to learn each other's quirks...and kinks. With the one-year anniversary of our first date looming, I ask him one night what he wants for a gift.

"For you to go clothes shopping with me," he says, as he's kissing me good night before taking off for his place across town.

I cock my head. Sam is not a shopper. He's a hot-looking guy, don't get me wrong, but there isn't a metrosexual bone in his body. He dresses appropriately for the occasion, but it's with the sense that clothing is an afterthought and he's throwing on whatever he knows is expected of him. I'd given him a couple of shirts and ties as gifts because I knew the colors would look good on him—and for his birthday I got him this gorgeous Irish wool sweater when I was on a work trip in Dublin, but beyond that, Sam takes care of his own clothing needs.

"For what?"

He shrugs, a sheepish grin creeping across his face. "Nothing special. Just...clothes shopping. Somewhere nice."

I sense this isn't about clothes shopping at all, but I play along. "Okay. When do you want to go?"

"Monday, lunchtime? Meet you at the mall?"

Clearly, he's thought about this and has a plan—a plan that he isn't ready to reveal. But this is Sam, the guy I'm very much in love with, and I trust him. So far. "Okay, Monday around twelve fifteen."

He's waiting for me outside of Nordstrom's on Monday. He looks sexy as hell, wearing the lavender shirt I bought him with the purple-and-navy-striped tie. I kiss him hard—a little surprised by how strong the emotion is. I love this guy. It's like, sometimes I forget that fact and then I see him and—boom!—it hits me again. I love him.

"Where do you want to start?" I ask, as he takes my arm and leads me toward the men's department.

"I have a confession," he murmurs in my ear as we maneuver between closely spaced racks of men's suits and toward tables of casual wear. "I got you here under false pretenses."

He says it so seriously, I have to laugh. "No kidding? Wow, I really thought you wanted to go clothes shopping. Okay, Mr. Secretive. Why are we here?"

He pulls me off the aisle and toward the dressing room. "There's something I want for our anniversary—something you do very, very well."

I can't help but blush because I know exactly what he's talking about. Every time we have sex—and I mean, *every* time—he says the same thing, after he's had a few minutes to catch his breath: "You do that very, very well." It's become something of a joke between us to the point that I now say the same thing after sex. And whenever we're in public or around friends and we want to let the other one know we're thinking about sex, we will make that comment about some totally nonsexual thing that someone is doing, like eating a hot dog at a backyard barbecue or setting up a tent for a group camping trip. It's usually a signal that we need to find some privacy immediately to engage in a little carnal knowledge.

"Really? A department-store dressing room?" I say, glancing

around the cubicle with its mirrored walls. I have to admit, it's a posh space to get it on in, with a cushy chair covered in expensive-looking silver fabric, but there's a problem. The door doesn't lock. It simply swings closed behind us.

"Sure, why not?" This is not the face of a man who loves clothes shopping. This is the face of a man who loves sex. With me. Who, in fact, loves me.

"What if someone walks in?"

"This place is empty. I only saw three people as we walked back here. "No one will walk in."

"Okay, but this isn't exactly a closed room," I whisper, gesturing toward the dressing-room walls that don't go all the way to the ceiling. "What if someone hears us and reports us? We could get arrested."

I wasn't entirely sure about that, whether we could actually get arrested or if a store manager would even press charges against us, but I had to say it. Because, quite frankly, I was totally game with whatever he wanted to do and I wanted to make sure he had thought the thing through before I turned my brain off and let my body—and his—take over.

"No one will hear," he says. "I'm very quiet during sex."

"But I'm not," I remind him, as if he needs reminding.

"Your mouth will be full."

"Fuck," I gasp. Just like that, my panties are soaked through. "Really?"

He nods, no trace of a smile on his face. It's just pure lust and I feel myself respond, leaning toward him, running my hands up his shoulders, pressing myself against his bulge.

"I'd better get to it, then," I manage, as I drop to my knees. What can I say? He gets to me.

"Wait a minute," he says, pulling me up again. "You'll be more comfortable in the chair."

"Such a gentleman." I sit in the chair and wait expectantly. He doesn't move toward me or unfasten his pants. "Well?"

"Let me see you."

I don't hesitate. It's not just that I want this as badly as he does, because I do, but that I'm also conscious of the time and the fact that the longer we linger, the more likely we are to get caught. I hike up my dress and spread my legs wide. My panties, a barely there shade of pink, are already wet and even I can see in the mirror the darker pink spot where the wetness has seeped through the fabric.

"Show me," he says, and there is a catch in his voice. "Take them off."

I lift my hips from the chair and shimmy out of my underwear, crossing my fingers that I don't leave a wet spot on the back of my dress. "There," I say, tossing the panties at him and letting him look his fill. "Now come here."

And he does, tucking my wet underwear in his shirt pocket. I reach for his belt and get it undone, then I make quick work of getting his pants open and freeing his erection. His dick, hard and ready, pops out at me like an amorous jack-in-the-box. I wet my lips and open my mouth around his girth. One last look at his lustful face and my eyes flutter closed. He loves my mouth and I love his dick—and right now, I don't give a damn about mirrors because I can feel everything that matters on the tip of my tongue.

He guides me by my hair, looping the length around his fist. I don't really need him to set the pace, I know what he likes and I know what he needs to get where he wants to go. Our rhythm is faster than the Muzak, I notice, before I'm completely lost in the sensation of him in my mouth, down my throat.

"Damn, baby, you look so amazing," he says and I know he's not only looking down at me, he's getting a view of this from every angle. "Touch yourself. I don't want to come alone."

I don't bother to argue, though I'm not sure I can suck him and also get myself off. But I slip my hand between my thighs and give it a try anyway. And what do you know, my clit is hungry for the attention. I gasp around him as I stroke myself, feeling as if he's the one doing it because he's still guiding me up and down his shaft and I'm keeping time with him. Within moments, I'm right there and tumbling over, coming on my fingers, moaning around his dick in my mouth, louder than I should be in a public place. But I don't care. I don't care if they drag me away in handcuffs because I'm coming and then he's coming and I'm gripping his thigh with one hand to keep from gagging while I still toy with my oversensitive clit. It's this strange moment in time, and we're suspended alone in a bubble. I moan louder than he does, even with my mouth full.

The moment couldn't be more perfect—and then someone knocks at the door.

"Do you need to try a different size?" a male voice asks.

The door squeaks as the salesman cracks it open and I freeze. Somehow, Sam has the sense to not only drag his pants up but to also step in front of the door, blocking it with his foot from being opened any farther.

"I'm good right now, thanks," he says, maybe a little too loudly, but sounding a lot more calm than I could manage at the moment. "I'll let you know."

The salesman murmurs something I can't hear and walks away. My hands are shaking as I stand up and smooth my dress down over my hips. I drag my fingers through the tangles in my hair while he straightens his clothes. Our eyes meet in the mirror.

"Happy Anniversary," I mouth, afraid to even whisper.

"You do that very, very well," he says, and suddenly we're both struck by a fit of the giggles.

Hands over our mouths, we try to stifle our laughs as we slip out of the dressing room and get lost in the tangle of men's sportswear. I grab his elbow as we make our escape from the mall and ask, "Hey, what did he say to you before he left?"

Sam casts a devilish look down the front of his shirt to my incriminating pink underwear still peeking out of his shirt pocket. "He said, 'Nice panties.'"

ABOUT THE AUTHORS

VIDA BAILEY (suffusedwithheat.blogspot.com) lives in Ireland. You can find her stories in Alison Tyler's *Big Book of Bondage* and *Sudden Sex* anthologies.

NEVE BLACK has been writing since she can remember and somewhere between studying the classics and earning a degree in English, she also discovered she enjoyed writing erotic stories.

Over the past ten years **CHEYENNE BLUE's** erotica has appeared in over seventy erotic anthologies and numerous websites. Visit her website at cheyenneblue.com.

JENNA BRIGHT (JennaBright.com and @Jenna_Bright on Twitter) loves writing erotic fiction that finds the sensual in the everyday.

RACHEL KRAMER BUSSEL (rachelkramerbussel.com and @raquelita on Twitter) has edited *Women in Lust, Orgasmic, Irresistible, Gotta Have It, Spanked, Suite Encounters, The Mile High Club* and other anthologies.

HEIDI CHAMPA (heidichampa.blogspot.com) is an extensively published erotic fiction author who resides in Pennsylvania.

LILY K. CHO (lilykcho@gmail.com) has collected erotica for twenty-five years, is a member of Mensa and thinks smart people are sexy!

ELIZABETH COLDWELL (elizabethcoldwell.wordpress. com) lives and writes in London. Her stories have appeared in numerous Cleis anthologies.

MARIPOSA CRUZ (mariposacruz.blogspot.com) writes, works and dances salsa in Reno, Nevada. Her writings include sexy shifter tales *Howl* and *Roar.*

CHRISTINE D'ABO (christinedabo.com) is hooked hard on romance. As a writer with over thirty publications, her imagination is always flowing.

MARTHA DAVIS (facebook.com/quixoticorchid or quixoticorchid@gmail.com) is an Atlanta writer of erotic romance and M/M fiction.

JEREMY EDWARDS (jeremeyedwardserotica.com) is the author of two erotocomedic novels and some 150 quirky, happy, sexy short stories.

EMERALD (thegreenlightdistrict.org and @Emerald_theGLD on Twitter) is an erotic fiction author and advocate for sexual freedom and authenticity.

AMY GLANCES lives in New York City and has a daily commute on the subway that provides endless inspiration for her creative fiction.

SACCHI GREEN (sacchi-green.blogspot.com) has edited eight erotica anthologies, including *Girl Fever* and the Lambda Literary Award–winner *Lesbian Cowboys*.

LOUISE HOOKER is a graduate of the University of North Alabama. A previous story of hers appeared in *Curvy Girls*. When not writing, she enjoys spending time with her fiancé of many years.

MICHAEL M. JONES (michaelmjones.com) is a writer, editor and reviewer. He is the editor of *Like A Cunning Plan: Erotic Trickster Tales*.

ANNABETH LEONG (annabethleong.blogspot.com and @AnnabethLeong on Twitter) once tried to count the statues at the Ten Thousand Buddhas Monastery.

A. J. LYLE (ajlyle.blogspot.com) lives in Canada and loves writing romantic erotica in her spare time.

RAELYNN MACDONALD is a young wife and proud mother, living in a small city in southern Ohio. She has a strong passion for writing and for exploring the erotic through her work.

NIKKI MAGENNIS (nikkimagennis.com) is an author and artist who lives in Scotland and has perfected the art of running away from reality.

SOMMER MARSDEN's (sommermarsden.blogspot.com) been called "...one of the top storytellers in the erotica genre" (Violet Blue) and "Unapologetic" (Alison Tyler). Her erotic novels include *Boys Next Door, Learning to Drown* and *Restless Spirit*.

CATHERINE PAULSSEN's (catherinepaulssen.com) stories have appeared in anthologies by Cleis Press, Silver Publishing, HarperCollins, Ravenous Romance and Constable & Robinson.

KELLY RAND (kellyrand.net or @rand_kelly on Twitter) is a Hamilton, Ontario-based writer and editor who dabbles in various erotic genres.

GISELLE RENARDE is a queer Canadian, avid volunteer, contributor to over one hundred short-story anthologies, and award-winning author of *Anonymous, Kinksters* and *My Mistress' Thighs*.

ANGELA R. SARGENTI's work appears in several anthologies. She has written four e-books, including *So Spankable*.

KATHLEEN TUDOR (kathleentudor.com or email PolyKathleen@gmail.com) has contributed to anthologies from Harper-Collins, Cleis, Storm Moon, Circlet, Xcite and more!

SASKIA WALKER's (saskiawalker.com and @SaskiaWalker on Twitter) erotic novels include *The Harlot*, *The Libertine* and *The Jezebel*. Saskia lives in Yorkshire with her real-life hero, Mark.

BRIGHTON WALSH (brightonwalsh.com) is a writer of steamy contemporary romance and lives out her fairytale in the Midwest with her husband and two kids.

ANYA M. WASSENBERG (anyawassenber.ca or @AnyaArts-Maven on Twitter) is a longtime freelance writer whose short fiction has been published in anthologies, periodicals and on the web in North America and the United Kingdom.

SALOME WILDE (salandtalerotica.com and @SalomeWilde on Twitter) has abundant pansexual erotica in print. She also writes M/M romance novels with Talon Rihai.

VERONICA WILDE (veronicawilde.com) is an erotic romance author whose work is published by Cleis Press, Liquid Silver Books and Samhain Publishing.

ROSALÍA ZIZZO is a hot-blooded Sicilian and former teacher whose work has appeared in various anthologies, including *Best Women's Erotica 2012* and *2013*.

ABOUT
THE EDITOR

Described by The Romance Reader as "a budding force to be reckoned with," **KRISTINA WRIGHT** (kristinawright.com) is a full-time writer and the editor of the bestselling *Fairy Tale Lust: Erotic Fantasies for Women*, as well as other Cleis Press anthologies including *Dream Lover: Paranormal Tales of Erotic Romance*; *Steamlust: Steampunk Erotic Romance*; *Lustfully Ever After: Fairy Tale Erotic Romance*; *Duty and Desire: Military Erotic Romance* and the *Best Erotic Romance* series. Kristina's erotica and erotic romance fiction has appeared in over one hundred anthologies and her articles, interviews and book reviews have appeared in numerous publications, both print and online. She received the Golden Heart Award for Romantic Suspense from Romance Writers of America for her first novel *Dangerous Curves* and she is a member of RWA as well as the special interest chapters Passionate Ink, and Fantasy, Futuristic and Paranormal. She holds degrees in English and humanities and has taught composition and world mythology at the college level. Originally from South Florida, Kristina is living happily ever after in Virginia with her husband Jay and their two little boys.

More from Kristina Wright

Best Erotic Romance
Edited by Kristina Wright

This year's collection is the debut of a new series! "Kristina is a phenomenal writer...she has the enviable ability to tell a story and simultaneously excite her readers."
—Erotica Readers and Writers Association
ISBN 978-1-57344-751-5 $14.95

Steamlust
Steampunk Erotic Romance
Edited by Kristina Wright

"Turn the page with me and step into the new worlds...where airships rule the skies, where romance and intellect are valued over money and social status, where lovers boldly discover each other's bodies, minds and hearts." —from the foreword by Meljean Brook
ISBN 978-1-57344-721-8 $14.95

Dream Lover
Paranormal Tales of Erotic Romance
Edited by Kristina Wright

Supernaturally sensual and captivating, the stories in *Dream Lover* will fill you with a craving that defies the rules of life, death and gravity. "...A choice of paranormal seduction for every reader. All are original and entertaining." —*Romantic Times*
ISBN 978-1-57344-655-6 $14.95

Fairy Tale Lust
Erotic Fantasies for Women
Edited by Kristina Wright

Award-winning novelist and erotica writer Kristina Wright goes over the river and through the woods to find the sexiest fairy tales ever written. "Deliciously sexy action to make your heart beat faster." —Angela Knight, the *New York Times* bestselling author of *Guardian*
ISBN 978-1-57344-397-5 $14.95

Lustfully Ever After
Fairy Tale Erotic Romance
Edited by Kristina Wright

Even grown-ups need bedtime stories, and this delightful collection of fairy tales will lead you down a magical path into forbidden romance and erotic love. The authors of *Lustfully Ever After* know your heart's most wicked and secret desires.
ISBN 978-1-57344-787-4 $14.95

Many More Than
Fifty Shades of Erotica

Please, Sir
Erotic Stories of Female Submission
Edited by Rachel Kramer Bussel

If you liked *Fifty Shades of Grey*, you'll love the explosive stories of *Yes, Sir*. These damsels delight in the pleasures of taking risks to be rewarded by the men who know their deepest desires. Find out why nothing is as hot as the power of the words "Please, Sir."
ISBN 978-1-57344-389-0 $14.95

Yes, Sir
Erotic Stories of Female Submission
Edited by Rachel Kramer Bussel

Bound, gagged or spanked—or controlled with just a glance—these lucky women experience the breathtaking thrills of sexual submission. *Yes, Sir* shows that pleasure is best when dispensed by a firm hand.
ISBN 978-1-57344-310-4 $15.95

He's on Top
Erotic Stories of Male Dominance and Female Submission
Edited by Rachel Kramer Bussel

As true tops, the bossy hunks in these stories understand that BDSM is about exulting in power that is freely yielded. These kinky stories celebrate women who know exactly what they want.
ISBN 978-1-57344-270-1 $14.95

Best Bondage Erotica 2013
Edited by Rachel Kramer Bussel

Let *Best Bondage Erotica 2013* be your kinky playbook to erotic restraint—from silk ties and rope to shiny cuffs, blindfolds and so much more. These stories of forbidden desire will captivate, shock and arouse you.
ISBN 978-1-57344-897-0 $15.95

Luscious
Stories of Anal Eroticism
Edited by Alison Tyler

Discover all the erotic possibilities that exist between the sheets and between the cheeks in this daring collection. "Alison Tyler is an author to rely on for steamy, sexy page turners! Try her!"—Powell's Books
ISBN 978-1-57344-760-7 $15.95

Happy Endings Forever And Ever

Dark Secret Love
A Story of Submission
By Alison Tyler

Inspired by her own BDSM exploits and private diaries, Alison Tyler draws on twenty-five years of penning sultry stories to create a scorchingly hot work of fiction, a memoir-inspired novel with reality at its core. A modern-day *Story of O*, a *9 1/2 Weeks*-style journey fueled by lust, longing and the search for true love.
ISBN 978-1-57344-956-4 $16.95

High-Octane Heroes
Erotic Romance for Women
Edited by Delilah Devlin

One glance and your heart will melt—these chiseled, brave men will ignite your fantasies with their courage and charisma. Award-winning romance writer Delilah Devlin has gathered stories of hunky, red-blooded guys who enter danger zones in the name of duty, honor, country and even love.
ISBN 978-1-57344-969-4 $15.95

Duty and Desire
Military Erotic Romance
Edited by Kristina Wright

The only thing stronger than the call of duty is the call of desire. *Duty and Desire* enlists a team of hot-blooded men and women from every branch of the military who serve their country and follow their hearts.
ISBN 978-1-57344-823-9 $15.95

Smokin' Hot Firemen
Erotic Romance Stories for Women
Edited by Delilah Devlin

Delilah delivers tales of these courageous men breaking down doors to steal readers' hearts! *Smokin' Hot Firemen* imagines the romantic possibilities of being held against a massively muscled chest by a man whose mission is to save lives and serve *every* need.
ISBN 978-1-57344-934-2 $15.95

Only You
Erotic Romance for Women
Edited by Rachel Kramer Bussel

Only You is full of tenderness, raw passion, love, longing and the many emotions that kindle true romance. The couples in *Only You* test the boundaries of their love to make their relationships stronger.
ISBN 978-1-57344-909-0 $15.95

Unleash Your Favorite Fantasies

The Big Book of Bondage
Sexy Tales of Erotic Restraint
Edited by Alison Tyler

Nobody likes bondage more than editrix Alison Tyler, who is fascinated with the ecstasies of giving up, giving in, and entrusting one's pleasure (and pain) into the hands of another. Delve into a world of unrestrained passion, where heart-stopping dynamics will thrill and inspire you.
ISBN 978-1-57344-907-6 $15.95

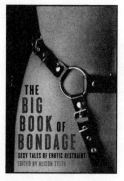

Hurts So Good
Unrestrained Erotica
Edited by Alison Tyler
Intricately secured by ropes, locked in handcuffs or bound simply by a lover's command, the characters of *Hurts So Good* find themselves in the throes of pleasurable restraint in this indispensible collection by prolific, award-winning editor Alison Tyler.
ISBN 978-1-57344-723-2 $14.95

Caught Looking
Erotic Tales of Voyeurs and Exhibitionists
Edited by Alison Tyler
and Rachel Kramer Bussel

These scintillating fantasies take the reader inside a world where people get to show off, watch, and feel the vicarious thrill of sex times two, their erotic power multiplied by the eyes of another.
ISBN 978-1-57344-256-5 $14.95

Hide and Seek
Erotic Tales of Voyeurs and Exhibitionists
Edited by Rachel Kramer Bussel
and Alison Tyler

Whether putting on a deliberate show for an eager audience or peeking into the hidden sex lives of their neighbors, these show-offs and shy types go all out in their quest for the perfect peep show.
ISBN 978-1-57344-419-4 $14.95

One Night Only
Erotic Encounters
Edited by Violet Blue

"Passion and lust play by different rules in *One Night Only*. These are stories about what happens when we have just that one opportunity to ask for what we want—and we take it… Enjoy the adventure."
—Violet Blue
ISBN 978-1-57344-756-0 $14.95

Red Hot Erotic Romance

Obsessed
Erotic Romance for Women
Edited by Rachel Kramer Bussel

These stories sizzle with the kind of obsession that is fueled by our deepest desires, the ones that hold couples together, the ones that haunt us and don't let go. Whether just-blooming passions, rekindled sparks or reinvented relationships, these lovers put the object of their obsession first.
ISBN 978-1-57344-718-8 $14.95

Passion
Erotic Romance for Women
Edited by Rachel Kramer Bussel

Love and sex have always been intimately intertwined—and *Passion* shows just how delicious the possibilities are when they mingle in this sensual collection edited by award-winning author Rachel Kramer Bussel.
ISBN 978-1-57344-415-6 $14.95

Girls Who Bite
Lesbian Vampire Erotica
Edited by Delilah Devlin

Bestselling romance writer Delilah Devlin and her contributors add fresh girl-on-girl blood to the pantheon of the paranormal. The stories in *Girls Who Bite* are varied, un-expected, and soul-scorching.
ISBN 978-1-57344-715-7 $14.95

Irresistible
Erotic Romance for Couples
Edited by Rachel Kramer Bussel

This prolific editor has gathered the most popular fantasies and created a sizzling, no-holds-barred collection of explicit encounters in which couples turn their deepest desires into reality.
978-1-57344-762-1 $14.95

Heat Wave
Hot, Hot, Hot Erotica
Edited by Alison Tyler

What could be sexier or more seductive than bare, sun-warmed skin? Bestselling erotica author Alison Tyler gathers explicit stories of summer sex bursting with the sweet eroticism of swimsuits, sprinklers, and ripe strawberries.
ISBN 978-1-57344-710-2 $15.95

Fuel Your Fantasies

Carnal Machines
Steampunk Erotica
Edited by D. L. King

In this decadent fusing of technology and romance, out-standing contemporary erotica writers use the enthralling possibilities of the 19th-century steam age to tease and titil-late.
ISBN 978-1-57344-654-9 $14.95

The Sweetest Kiss
Ravishing Vampire Erotica
Edited by D. L. King

These sanguine tales give new meaning to the term "dead sexy" and feature beautiful bloodsuckers whose desires go far beyond blood.
ISBN 978-1-57344-371-5 $15.95

The Handsome Prince
Gay Erotic Romance
Edited by Neil Plakcy

A bawdy collection of bedtime stories brimming with classic fairy tale characters, reimagined and recast for any man who has dreamt of the day his prince will come. These sexy stories fuel fantasies and remind us all of the power of true romance.
ISBN 978-1-57344-659-4 $14.95

Daughters of Darkness
Lesbian Vampire Tales
Edited by Pam Keesey

"A tribute to the sexually aggressive wom-an and her archetypal roles, from nurturing goddess to dangerous predator."
—*The Advocate*
ISBN 978-1-57344-233-6 $14.95

Dark Angels
Lesbian Vampire Erotica
Edited by Pam Keesey

Dark Angels collects tales of lesbian vam-pires, the quintessential bad girls, archetypes of passion and terror. These tales of desire are so sharply erotic you'll swear you've been bitten!
ISBN 978-1-57344-252-7 $13.95

* Free book of equal or lesser value. Shipping and applicable sales tax extra.
Cleis Press • (800) 780-2279 • orders@cleispress.com
www.cleispress.com

Read the Very Best in Erotica

Fairy Tale Lust
Erotic Fantasies for Women
Edited by Kristina Wright
Foreword by Angela Knight

Award-winning novelist and top erotica writer Kristina Wright goes over the river and through the woods to find the sexiest fairy tales ever written.
ISBN 978-1-57344-397-5 $14.95

In Sleeping Beauty's Bed
Erotic Fairy Tales
By Mitzi Szereto

"Classic fairy tale characters like Rapunzel, Little Red Riding Hood, Cinderella, and Sleeping Beauty, just to name a few, are brought back to life in Mitzi Szereto's delightful collection of erotica fairy tales."
—Nancy Madore, author of *Enchanted: Erotic Bedtime Stories for Women*
ISBN 978-1-57344-376-8 $16.95

Frenzy
60 Stories of Sudden Sex
Edited by Alison Tyler

"Toss out the roses and box of candies. This isn't a prolonged seduction. This is slammed against the wall in an alleyway sex, and it's all that much hotter for it."
—Erotica Readers & Writers Association
ISBN 978-1-57344-331-9 $14.95

Fast Girls
Erotica for Women
Edited by Rachel Kramer Bussel

Fast Girls celebrates the girl with a reputation, the girl who goes all the way, and the girl who doesn't know how to say "no."
ISBN 978-1-57344-384-5 $14.95

Can't Help the Way That I Feel
Sultry Stories of African American Love, Lust and Fantasy
Edited by Lori Bryant-Woolridge

Some temptations are just too tantalizing to ignore in this collection of delicious stories edited by Emmy award-winning and *Essence* bestselling author Lori Bryant-Woolridge.
ISBN 978-1-57344-386-9 $14.95

Ordering is easy! Call us toll free or fax us to place your MC/VISA order.
You can also mail the order form below with payment to:
Cleis Press, 2246 Sixth St., Berkeley, CA 94710.

ORDER FORM .

QTY	TITLE	PRICE
___	_____	_____
___	_____	_____
___	_____	_____
___	_____	_____
___	_____	_____
___	_____	_____
___	_____	_____
___	_____	_____

SUBTOTAL _____

SHIPPING _____

SALES TAX _____

TOTAL _____

Add $3.95 postage/handling for the first book ordered and $1.00 for each additional book. Outside North America, please contact us for shipping rates. California residents add 9% sales tax. Payment in U.S. dollars only.

★ Free book of equal or lesser value. Shipping and applicable sales tax extra.

Cleis Press • Phone: (800) 780-2279 • Fax: (510) 845-8001
orders@cleispress.com • www.cleispress.com
You'll find more great books on our website

Follow us on Twitter @cleispress • Friend/fan us on Facebook